A

THERE IS TRUTH

STORM

TO ANY STORY.

OF

DETAILS DON'T MATTER.

STORIES

award-winning author

K.B. JENSEN

A Storm of Stories

Published by Crimson Cloud Media LLC.

Chicago, IL

FIC019000 FICTION / Literary

ISBN: 978-0-692-66094-2

Cover by Shira Lee Designs, copyright owned by K.B. Jensen

www.kbjensenauthor.com

To my great loves, K.S. and A.M.S., as well as my family and friends. I count you among the stars.

CHAPTER 1
THE BREAKDOWN

The windshield wipers slapped in a steady rhythm. The radio had turned to fuzz and whistles, like it was on the same station as the rest of reality. It's called a whiteout for a reason, and the wind was whipping the white stuff around like crazy. She was going forty miles an hour, and she couldn't see much beyond the tiny, yellow circle of her headlights in the dark. All it showed was white on County Road Z. She hunched forward over the steering wheel with her shoulders close to her ears. Her stomach did flips every time the tires started to slide and lose their grip on the road.

"Don't go out of the grooves," she said out loud to herself. "It's going to be okay. Just another twenty miles to go. You should've known it was going to blizzard. It's January in Wisconsin. You need to start watching the forecast." She heard her father's voice ringing with that last thought.

She always talked to herself in the car. People at stoplights probably thought she was crazy, but she didn't care. "Crap," she muttered.

She saw a dark figure ahead of her with a pair of arms raised, and she slammed on the brakes. The car seemed to float, like a boat moving across water. There was no friction, just a sliding sensation and a slow motion spinning out until the car was perpendicular to the road. Its front had slammed into a snow bank. The impact had swung her head forward and back and sent everything loose in the car flying, including her cell phone.

She got out and there he was lying in the snow bank, a hitch-hiker maybe judging by his tattered coat. He wasn't moving, just lying on the ground with his arms and legs under him. His face was out of view. Worried he might be hurt or worse, she ran over to him, her dress shoes crunching on the snow. Her hands were shaking as she grabbed at his coat and shook his shoulder. She was relieved to see a smile appear on his face.

"You're an angel," he said, gasping. "Thank God you stopped. No one else was stopping. I was freezing to death."

"I could've killed you," she stuttered. "You sure you're okay?"

"I'm fine," he said. "At least I think I'm fine. You didn't hit me very fast. It felt like more of a knock. I kind of rolled." He patted himself down as if to make sure he still had all his limbs and winced slightly as he leaned forward.

"I'm so glad you're okay," she said. "But you shouldn't have jumped in front of my car like that. What the hell were you think-ing? You could've been killed."

"Would you have stopped if I hadn't?" he asked. "I'm freezing to death out here."

"I would've stopped," she said. "If I had seen you." She wondered if this was true. Stopping for strangers on the side of the road wasn't something she usually did, but a snowstorm was different wasn't it? It could be a matter of life or death. She would have had to make the decision in a matter of seconds, and she wondered what she would have chosen.

"Doubt it," he said, as if he were reading her mind. "But I'm glad you're here now. Can I have a ride?"

"Sure," she said and then turned and looked at her car. The hood of the little, white Mazda was dug deep into the snow bank. The car was facing down into the ditch at an angle, which wouldn't help when it came time to pull out.

"Shit," she said. "Can you dig me out of that?"

They tried until they were both coated in white powder. She tried hacking with a scraper against the icy mound, then used her gloves to scoop out the snow, but the car was too far in. He bent down and tried to dig out around the wheels. Her feet were numb and her hands were freezing, but they had barely made a dent in the snowdrift. The snow had colored her blond hair white and she could feel it dampening her hair.

"This isn't working," she muttered, wiping the snow out of her eyes. It was hard to see.

She brushed as much of the snow and ice off as she could before she got back in the car, then shook it out of her hair, and slammed the driver's side door shut. There he was on the passenger side.

Without the blur of snow clouding her vision she noticed he was actually kind of beautiful in a dirty hippie sort of way. Under his gray, wool hat, he had long waves of reddish brown hair and a set of deep, blue eyes. He was the kind of guy you want to take home and give a bath. It was hard to tell how old he was in the dark, maybe in his thirties. He looked at her like he was expecting something, and she snapped back into focus.

"We should call triple A," she said. "Or the cops. We could call the cops for help, right?"

"That's a great idea," he said.

She fumbled for her phone among the debris in the console and swore when she saw it was cracked. Her fingers were icy cold but they fiddled with the buttons. It didn't turn on. It was a useless piece of plastic with a black, blank screen. The thing had flown out of the cup holder when she slammed on the brakes and hit the dashboard.

"What about you? You got a phone?"

He shook his head and she wondered what kind of person wanders around in a whiteout without a phone. She wondered what kind of person wanders around in a whiteout at all.

"What were you doing out there?" she asked.

"I broke down…" he said.

"Where's your car?" she asked.

"I don't know," he said.

"Are you homeless?" she blurted out.

"Does it matter?" he asked.

"Guess not," she said, taking a few deep breaths. It was a shallow question, she realized, but she was still rattled. Her hands were still shaking. She wondered if she should be afraid of him.

"What about you?" he asked. "What the hell are you doing out here?"

"I was on my way home from class in Madison after work," she said. "I'm getting my M.B.A. in an evening program. My parents live in the middle of nowhere and I live with them right now. How about you? What do you do?"

"I'm a jack-of-all-trades," he said, laughing. "I'm a waiter, a bus boy, an artist, a pickpocket, a sailor and a psychic." He raised an eyebrow.

"Let me tell you your future," he said with a grin.

She couldn't help but laugh nervously as she let him take the wet glove off her hand to examine her damp palm. His gloves were tucked near the heater vent on the dashboard. She wanted to pull her hand away, but he pulled it forward.

There was a small tickle of electricity as he traced the lifeline on her palm with his pointer finger. But then he recoiled and started shaking.

"I'm sorry," he said. "I can't tell you your future."

"Why not?" she asked, pulling her hand back and crossing her arms. She leaned away from him.

"Because you can't tell the future of the people whose destinies run close to yours." As the words came out of his lips, she noticed he had a small gap between his front teeth. The words made her shiver, not because they were eerie but because she suspected they were true.

The windshield wipers were still slapping and she wondered how much gas she had left. She was afraid to look. She was afraid of a lot of things. Who was this stranger? Would they freeze to death? Would someone crash into them? She put the car in reverse and let the tires spin for a few minutes. They whirred loudly. The Mazda shuddered, but it did not budge. She gave up and put it back into neutral but left the car running.

She leaned her seat back and he leaned his seat back. She stared at him in the dark for a moment, his blue eyes glittering back at her in the shadows. It made her think of the way the moonlight catches on a snow bank, specks glittering like diamonds. She looked out the window, wishing she could see the moon, but all she saw was white and black, night and snow.

"My parents must be so worried," she whispered.

"I've got a headache," he said, with his eyebrows furrowed.

"You can sleep if you want to," she said, trying to comfort him.

"I don't feel like sleeping yet," he said. "Why don't you sleep?"

He was looking at her, and she had no intention of sleeping with his eyes on her like that. His eyes were dilated in the dark, with large black pupils rimmed by light blue. I don't trust you, she thought. I don't make a habit of trusting strange men I don't know who jump in front of my car. Like hell, I'll sleep. But she was more diplomatically Midwestern than that.

"I can't sleep. I've got to clear the tailpipe of snow so we don't get carbon monoxide poisoning, wipe off the brake lights so no one slams into us and turn the car on and off to conserve gas," she said in a monotone voice.

"How do you know all this?" he asked.

"I saw a survival show on TV," she said. "Discovery Channel, I think."

"What else did you learn?" he asked, holding his head and wincing slightly.

"That I should've put a fucking chocolate bar in the car."

"Too bad on the chocolate," he said.

Her stomach growled loudly on cue. She was thirsty too and eyed the white stuff outside. If it melted on her tongue, would it quench the thirst or make it worse? She wondered and then remembered it would only make it worse.

"But I do have a sleeping bag in my car, at least," she said. "That's another thing they say you should have. My dad always insisted."

She reached to the back seat and grabbed for the sleeping bag. It was green and earthy smelling with a few flecks of dirt dotting the slinky fabric. It had been in the car for a long time. She unwound it and spread it out evenly over the driver and passenger sides. It made her feel safer to be under something warm, strangely enough, even though he was under it too. The windshield was covered in a white blanket, and so were the car's sides. It felt like the world was shrinking, encased in whiteness.

"We could get hit from behind," he said.

"I know."

"We could die tonight," he said.

"I know," she said, as calmly as she could. Her heart was starting to pound.

"Maybe that's why I can't read your fortune," he said. "Because we're going to die together."

His eyes were wide and fearful, and she almost wanted to reach out and pat him on the arm, but she didn't. She was still afraid of him.

"We should do something to pass the time," she said. "Take our minds off things."

He smiled real big when she said that, a little too big.

"Please, I barely know you," she said. She wished she could kick him out of the car just then, but where would he go? Where would she go? There was nothing but white-streaked darkness outside the car.

"It could be our last night on earth," he said.

"You're so cliché," she said. "No way." She gritted her teeth.

"You're gonna change your mind," he said, the smile still there. "I have a feeling you're gonna sleep with me before the night's over."

"Like hell I will," she said, leaning away from him.

His hand twitched on his thigh and she could see his fingers gripping his leg, the white knuckles. He loosened his grip and she could see his hands were shaking. Maybe he was actually scared. Scared or angry?

Her leg was starting to bounce around involuntarily. The tension in the car was setting it off. She needed to collect herself so she put on gloves and stepped out of the Mazda. The snow flew into her eyes. She opened her mouth and snow flew in. But the drops melting did nothing for her thirst, and she closed her mouth again. She scraped the snow off the brake lights, shining red against white, and cleaned out the dirty mouth of the tailpipe, oil staining her gloves.

When she stepped back into the car, his eyes were closed, and she thought for a moment, it's safe to sleep now, maybe, for a little while. The clock on the car read 10:33 p.m. in glowing green digits. She would normally be tired. She turned off the engine. The cold would wake her up. But she couldn't sleep because she had a stranger in her car, and her heart was still pounding. They needed help.

She heard his voice whisper in the dark, "What did you have in mind then, to pass the time?"

And she looked over at the blue eyes in the dark.

"Stories," she said. "We could tell each other stories."

"Confess all our sins?" he asked.

"Well, I wasn't thinking that extreme," she said. "But maybe it's not a bad idea."

"I killed a man," he said.

She opened her mouth and let out a slow breath, the kind an animal makes when it freezes in front of a predator. Her eyes opened wide in the bright snowlight. What else do you call the mix of swirling white snow, moon and blackness outside? Snowlight.

And then he started laughing. "I haven't even told you my

name yet," he said. "And you think I'm going to make that kind of confession."

So he turned on his side like he was going to sleep, and she stared at the back of his coat. It was brown and tattered and reminded her of a camel. The collar had remnants of what must have once been fur.

The collar was waterlogged. The ice and snow crusted to the coat had started to melt. She could see the trickles sliding down his back in dark ripples. He must be cold, she thought. He must be. Because she was, so she turned on the ignition and there was the soft sound of the Mazda purring. She could smell the gas. The windshield wipers scraped against the ice, and the windows were fogged and dripping wet with condensation. She turned up the defroster. I don't care if it wakes him, she thought, because he's playing games with me, and I hate that.

"What kind of person says they killed someone just to get a rise out of a stranger," she muttered. "Who does that?"

"Someone looking to pass the time, maybe," he said.

"Well, it's kind of fucked up," she said. "Are you trying to freak me out? It's scary enough picking up somebody on the side of the road."

Now it was hot and he was still shivering. With the hot air blowing on them, her feet were sweating inside her dress shoes. She had tossed the whole sleeping bag to his side.

"How can you be so cold?" she asked.

"I got wet," he said. "What do the survival shows say about that?"

"It's a bad thing," she said.

"Why don't you take your jacket off and air out a bit?" she said.

"I don't want to," he said, pulling up his collar.

"So why are you out here?" she asked.

"I told you, I had a breakdown," he said.

"So where is your car?"

"What car?" he said, laughing. "Hey, shouldn't you be watching the gas?"

"Yes," she said in an exasperated tone and turned off the engine. His responses were getting frustrating. They didn't make any sense.

They both watched the needle slide down, as she turned the engine off. It went down from less than a quarter tank to orange to red, like a preview. This is what's going to happen over the next few hours, she thought.

"I think we should cuddle," he said.

She looked at him for a minute. If it were just a matter of appearances alone, snuggling with him would not be a problem, she thought. But he kept messing with her.

"I don't trust you," she said.

"I wouldn't trust me either," he said. "But what do the survival shows say anyway?"

"They say I should have a working cell phone," she said, running her thumb along the cracked screen, and then pressing the power button. The phone was unresponsive.

"Who would you call?" he asked.

"My boyfriend," she said. "I'm sure he's worried."

"You don't have a boyfriend," he said with a smirk.

"Yes, I do," she said a little too loud. She shifted her body away from him, uncomfortable in the seat, uncomfortable in the conversation.

"Nope," he said. "I'm a psychic, remember? You wouldn't be so wound up, if you had a boyfriend. It's your mother."

"Do I need to kick you out of my car?" she said.

"Depends," he said. "Are you a heartless bitch?"

"Maybe."

"You'd be willing to kill me because I have bad manners?" he asked. "Interesting."

"Just trying to pass the time," she said. This time she laughed, and he didn't.

She closed her eyes and heard his breath slow down, gradually rise and fall rhythmically in waves that reminded her of the ocean. Her breath and heart slowed down too until she was walking on the beach alongside him, and it was warm and sunny. They were holding hands. The sleep was impossible to resist. Her heart had beaten so long and so hard, had been so wound up and whipped up with the snow, that it wasn't a choice anymore but an involuntary reaction.

And here we are in the sunshine. No, she thought. This isn't real. But here we are skipping stones along the water. Here we are dipping our feet into the foamy waves, over and over in the sea salty warmth. "How did we get here again?" he asked.

"I don't know," she said in the dream.

When she awoke, there he was with his tangle of reddish brown hair cascading across the seat.

"I have to trust you," she said. "That's what the survival books say."

And so she climbed over the armrest and wrapped her arms around the damp, brown jacket. She brushed his hair to the side so it wasn't in her face. Her legs lined up with his legs. It was an odd pairing, like the wrong kind of food with the wrong kind of wine.

"I told you you'd sleep with me," he said softly.

And just as she started to get comfortable, just as the shivering seemed to have slowed down, that's when she noticed the blood. It had soaked through the back of his jacket. It was hot and sticky and congealed against her shaking fingers.

The sight of his blood made her stomach lurch. Her heart pumped her own blood through her veins in an uneasy, fast-paced rhythm. She could feel her heart clunking away sloppily through it all, like it was going to sink in her chest, another piece of faulty machinery in a broken down car. Up to this moment, she had been upbeat and hopeful that help would come soon enough. Now she wasn't so sure.

"Oh my God," she yelled. "You *are* hurt. I'm so sorry." The features of her face squeezed together as if the tears would rush out of her eyes any minute. But they didn't. She fought to blink them back. Crying wouldn't help anything. It would not make him feel any better, and she didn't want him to panic. "It's my fault, isn't it? I'm the one who hit you," she mumbled. "Fuck."

"How bad is it?" he asked. "Is there a lot of blood?"

"Not that much," she lied. "It will be okay. It's... it's not that bad."

"My head does ache, but it's not the first time," he said.

"Are you delirious?" she asked. "Have you been delirious the whole time?"

"I never had any intention of shooting anyone," he said. "They shot first."

"Hush now," she said. "You don't know what you're saying."

He had a concussion, she thought. He was in shock. She pulled back his collar and saw it was not water that had melted along the back of his jacket but blood. The color had been hard to make out in the dark. She pulled back his hair, and she could see the small wound, a gash at the base of his skull with its edges puckered. It must have started as a tiny trickle of blood at first, but as the time had passed the inside of his jacket had become wet, the collar soaked. He yawned.

"You might have a concussion," she said. "You shouldn't sleep."

"Is that what the survival shows say?" he said, shivering. "Screw it, I'm going to sleep."

"No," she said. "You can't. "You have to stay awake."

She opened her jacket and tore a piece of her T-shirt off underneath her sweater and held it against the base of his skull. The blood gushed warm into the white cotton. Her fingers were sticky and wet. She was angry with herself for not noticing she'd hurt him. How do you not notice a head wound? What if he died?

"Now that you pointed it out, it does hurt like a bitch," he said. "Distract me."

"You want a story?" she asked.

"You and your stories," he said. "Tell me something juicy, or I'm going to fall asleep."

"Okay, I think I know how to keep a man awake. So Mr. Psychic, what do you think about this one?

"There once was a girl who was a nymphomaniac. She figured it out when she was fifteen, and a boy made her toes curl so hard they cramped up.

'How often would you want to have sex?' the girl asked him.

'Once a week,' the boy said.

'That's it?' she said.

'How about you?' the boy said.

'Everyday,' the girl said, watching his eyes widen. Ahh, she was a freak, wasn't she, she thought. And so she made this rule early on, a rather old-fashioned one."

"What was the rule?" the dying hitchhiker asked, perking up.

"Never fuck a man you don't love."

"Then you aren't really a nymphomaniac," he said.

"It's a made-up story," she said, blushing in the dark. Why couldn't she think of a better story? A real story about a safe topic, a boring, normal topic.

He laughed. "Sure. You know, if you were a man, you'd just be called a man. No one would think anything of it."

"It's not fair, is it?" she said. "I guess it's just a label. Fuck labels."

"So you aren't going to be granting a dying man any last wishes, then?" he asked.

"Nope," she said. "Not unless you make me fall in love with you in a couple of hours."

"That's impossible," he said, starting to close his eyes. "Impossible love. Why don't you tell me some stories about that?"

"I don't know about love but I can tell you impossible stories," she said, dabbing at the back of his head. She examined the wound again. It was ripe and raw with a flap of skin spewing wine-colored liquid in the dark. What did the survival shows say? Keep him awake. Go outside, find a dead reindeer carcass and feed him pieces from it. Oh, those fucking shows. Press down on the wound. The cotton was dripping. "It's the least I can do since I almost killed you," she said. "I don't know what the hell the stories will be about, though. All I can think about is the fact I nearly killed you."

"It's not your fault, you know," he said. "I jumped in front of your car. Besides, it's nicer to bleed to death inside a warm car than freeze to death out in the cold."

"Actually, the survival shows say freezing to death isn't so bad," she said. "You just go numb and get sleepy."

"I always mess these things up, even my own death," he said, smiling. "At least I get to look at someone beautiful as I bleed to death. Turn the engine on, please."

"It's already on," she said.

His head slumped forward and she slapped him gently. "Wake up, now. If you've got a concussion, I don't want you sleeping. They'll find us soon enough. You can sleep in the hospital."

He moaned and closed his eyes.

"I'm so sorry," she said. "I thought you were crazy. I didn't know you were bleeding."

"Maybe I am crazy," he said. "Why should it matter?"

She leaned forward against the dashboard and heaved a sob or two before collecting herself. The fear ratcheted up in her stomach, tightened in her abdomen, squeezed her chest and spilled out of her mouth in a series of short, tight gasps.

"I've made this drive a million times. It's only sixty miles," she said. "I should've just skipped class."

"Maybe you should go get help?" he said.

"And where am I going to walk to? This is a rural area in the middle of fucking Wisconsin. There's not a barn or a house within ten miles of here. I know this road. We just have to stay with the car," she said. "That's what we're supposed to do, stay with the car."

"Oh, my head," he said, his hand cradling his skull. "Worst headache of my life. Distract me, please. Please just distract me."

"Did I ever tell you the story of the dog?" she said. "Of course not. We've never met before this."

"It feels like we have," he said. "I think I've known you a long time, since we were children."

That doesn't make any sense, she thought. The poor man isn't making any sense anymore. Did he ever make sense? Why was he walking in the middle of a snowstorm? The wind roared outside, shaking the car slightly.

"What were you doing out there walking around?" she asked.

"I don't remember," he said. "Why were you driving?"

"I told you I had to get home," she said.

"A sixty-mile commute. Environmental karma. Your carbon footprint must be horrendous," he said, leaning back his head and wincing. He seemed to go in and out in terms of coherency. Sometimes she'd swear he was normal. She wondered if he could be faking it, but then again, she could see the wound as clear as day.

She ripped off another piece of her T-shirt and dabbed the back of his head and his neck. Her stomach felt exposed under her sweater and coat. She just pushed the cotton against the mouth of the wound. The bleeding seemed to have slowed. He moaned. She rubbed his back with her other hand.

"Has anyone ever told you the story about the dog?" she said. "The St. Bernard?"

"No," he said. "Why, does it matter?"

"It's a true story," she said. "A friend of a friend swore it was true. His friend was babysitting this guy's St. Bernard while he was on vacation, and the dog died."

"Oh no," he said.

"And it was a record hot Chicago summer and the thing instantly started to rot and stink in the heat. She called the vet offices to find out how much it would cost to cremate the poor thing. The cheapest place was $200 bucks. She was a student, so she didn't have any money or a car, but she was gonna put it on a credit card."

"Why didn't she call the owner?" he asked.

"She tried, but she couldn't get a hold of him."

He leaned back his seat some more and closed his eyes, picturing the giant dead dog and this scrawny, blond girl in his head.

"Then what?" he asked. He took a broken breath.

"So she has no way to transport it. The dog weighs hundreds of pounds and she stuffs it in a huge suitcase and can't even close the zipper all the way. One of its paws is sticking out, and she keeps trying to push it back in. She wheels the suitcase to the Brown Line train station. But the station has no elevator and she's struggling up the steep, narrow, wooden steps."

He opened his eyes and there they were at the bottom of the steps and the petite, blond girl with the wavy hair was pulling this suitcase up, step by step, walking backward, her back hunched over, her thin arms stretched out like her elbows were going to pop from the strain.

"And this guy offers to help her. 'Thank God,' she says. 'Thanks so much.' He carries it up and they get to the top a split second before the train pulls away, and he darts inside. The doors slide shut, and she watches him pull away with the suitcase with the dead dog. He was a thief. He stole the dog. And she's left there wondering, shit how am I gonna explain this to the owner. He's never going to believe me."

"That didn't happen," he said, shaking his head and then wincing from the pain. "Come on. That's impossible."

"Maybe the details are sketchy, but there's still some truth to it," she insisted. "It did happen. And imagine the thief, what he must have thought when he opened the suitcase and found a dead dog."

"I can imagine," he said.

"You know why I'm telling you this story?" she said. "A week ago, my cousin from Mississippi told me the same goddamn story. I kid you not."

"What happened to the dog?" he asked.

"I like to think he's been traveling," she said.

"All the way to Mississippi and back," he said.

"Yeah, you get it," she said, smiling. "No one ever gets my stories."

Then he slipped off into unconsciousness for a while and she let him stay in the land of dreams. She hoped she didn't let him stay there a little too long. She tapped her foot nervously and then stopped, worried about bothering him.

"Have you ever stolen anything?" she whispered in the dark when she saw his eyes open.

"Yes," he said. "I've stolen a few hearts."

She rolled her eyes and then remembered he was hurting. She hoped he hadn't seen her reaction in the dark. It was unkind and she knew it. She rubbed his sleeve and the fabric felt cold. Her fingers were cold in her gloves, their tips going numb. The gas was getting lower and lower so she didn't turn the engine on. Their breath rose like clouds, twirled and evaporated then rained down along the windows in streaks. She couldn't help but draw on the windows with her fingertip, anything to pass the time. Help, she wrote. Help!!! No one would ever read a sign in condensation. No one would ever notice it. But it felt like a cosmic message she was sending across the universe, nothing fancy, just another prayer really.

"I'm going to die, aren't I?" he said.

"No, you aren't," she said. "Not in my car."

"Would that be impolite?" he mumbled.

"Yes, you've got to live so you can pay for my upholstery cleaning bill," she said dryly.

He didn't laugh. "Of course," he said. "I'll pay for that."

"I'm just kidding," she said, grimacing. "I'm sorry, I have a knack for saying the wrong thing at the wrong time. What the hell is wrong with me?"

"Nothing," he said. "Maybe it wasn't a bad thing to say. It's true. Your upholstery is ruined. And what's wrong with feeling a sense of earthly obligation? Maybe it will keep me here for a while."

"You talk kind of funny for a sick man," she said.

The upholstery was all black anyway and the car wasn't exactly new. The blood would never even show.

"I am a learn-ed man," he said, smiling. "At least I was once, in a past life."

She smiled, and he winced suddenly, like a knife had been twisted into him.

"I'm in so much pain," he said. "No one ever seems to notice."

"I've noticed. I'm sorry," she said.

"What are you studying?" he asked, changing the subject.

"Accounting," she said, involuntarily making a face.

"Respectable profession. Why the face?"

"I'd rather be a writer." She sighed.

The wind whistled outside the car. She pulled the sleeping bag up higher against her neck.

"Then why don't you?" he asked.

"Everyone tells me I'd starve," she said.

"Maybe you would," he said. "But you could always marry well." He laughed.

"Maybe," she laughed. "But there's one other problem. I never share my stories."

"Why not?"

"I'm afraid everyone will think I'm crazy."

"Maybe you are," he said. "Nothing wrong with that. I like crazy women. I can relate to them."

He smiled, and she smiled, and he grimaced again.

"I like to tell stories," he said. "How do you come up with a story?"

"I daydream it," she said. "I just sit and daydream it, and it plays like a reel in my head. I can see the characters sitting and talking to each other. I can hear the dialogue like a play or a movie. The edges are blurry. It's a rough sketch, maybe I don't know what the furniture looks like, or the color of the kitchen counter or the color of someone's eyes, but I love to dream up a story. It's a great escape."

"You ever have nightmares?" he asked, taking her gloved hand and holding it in his own. She nodded. He squeezed her hand tightly. There was no warmth between them. There was too much fabric.

"I used to have nightmares that I'd been shot in the neck," he said. "I'd call 911 for help and the dispatcher would tell me, 'You're not really hurt, you're fine, you're going to be okay, you can still talk.' I'd ask my parents and friends for help and they'd all say the same thing. You'll be fine. I'd just keep wandering and bleeding and asking for help, and no one would listen until finally my brain had had enough of the torture and told me to wake up."

"I'm sorry I didn't notice earlier," she said. "You haven't been shot. You're going to be fine. You're going to be okay."

"I know," he said. "I'm still talking, aren't I?"

She was quiet after he said that. She had said the wrong thing again, hadn't she? She had lied to him just like the people in his dreams, and what's worse than a lie?

"Tell me one of your stories," he said.

She sat there, her breath rising, her chest rising, trying to think of something. One character or another flashed through her head, a line here or there. She'd have to tell it on her feet. She wasn't good at telling stories on her feet, she thought. She was nervous. Something about telling a story was like taking off her clothes, and he was a stranger. But what the hell, it wasn't like he was going to remember judging by the state of his head. He might not even live. Her chest was tight. Her shoulders were tight from the cold.

"Okay, this story isn't true…" she said.

"Of course not," he said, rolling his eyes.

"Let me get started," she said, trying to buy time.

"Hurry up," he said. "I have a bad feeling we're going to die at four a.m."

"Four a.m., really? On the spot?" she laughed. "I'll keep an eye on the clock."

She probably should've been more frightened. "I know it's silly, but I've always thought I can't die until I finish writing my book," she said quietly. "I've got to stick around."

"Is that so," he said. "I didn't know writing was a ticket to immortality. Maybe I should take it up."

"I don't know about immortality," she said. "Maybe if you get famous, but I never will."

"Why not?" he asked, leaning his head gingerly back against the headrest.

"My stories aren't that good."

"Ah, a writer without an ego. Why don't you let me be the judge of that," he said. "Tell me a few. Come on. To pass the time."

"Do you think it would be better if I tried to go get help?" she said. She reached for the handle on the door.

"I don't want you to leave me alone," he said, pulling her back. "Besides, what do the survival shows say?"

"To stay with the car," she said softly. She was trying to convince herself it was the right answer. It was eerily quiet. She waited for the whoosh of a car going past but there was nothing, just the howling of the wind.

"Tell me a story about a taboo," he said dreamily. "Tell me a story about something no one talks about. Tell me a story about something you don't know a damn thing about."

He had beautiful eyes, she thought. It was hard to see them in the dark, blue and deep in the pale snowlight. There it was again, silver and pale. The snow had let up. Now the wind was blowing wisps of snowdrifts around the car. It felt like they were moving, but they were still. His eyes were starting to close again and she lightly shook him.

"Have you ever traveled?" she asked.

"Not much," he said. "You?"

"I studied abroad for a year, traveled all over the world, even went to India. I used up most of my college savings that way, went into debt... my parents were ecstatic. I never did get a decent paying job after undergrad. Now I live at home."

"Let's go to India," he mumbled. "Let's get on a plane together."

"You're crazy," she laughed nervously.

"No, you are," he mumbled. "I'm falling asleep again. I'm cold. Just hold me, and tell me a story. Just tell me something, my friend, anything."

His chest shuddered involuntarily.

"Okay, okay," she said. "Hush now and don't interrupt. I'll lose my train of thought."

He nodded, and she began in a soft, shaky voice.

CHAPTER 2
AMERICAN ON THE PLANE

I f she had known the heartache it would cause, she would not have taken the $200 voucher and the first class upgrade to switch from an overbooked flight. But at the time it had seemed like a good idea. So what if it meant waiting around for two more hours? It was almost midnight anyway, and she had a fourteen-hour flight from Chicago to Delhi to look forward to. Her fiancé and India could wait a few hours more.

While seated at the gate, she noticed a blond man staring at her. She looked away and gazed at the planes sitting outside the window in the dark and at the luggage being tossed into the plane's hold under the yellow lights. Lately, she felt like a suitcase being thrown about, never sure where she'd end up. Her fiancé had an excellent job lined up in Delhi, a once-in-a-lifetime opportunity. She didn't. But it was a chance to go home for good, and he was worth the trip back. Though she always called it home, she hadn't lived in India since she was eight years old.

She glanced up again at the slim, blond man with the blue eyes. She was raven haired with a dark, golden complexion and filled out her American blue jeans with an hourglass figure. The only hint of India on her was a thick, gold bangle dangling off her right wrist. It was something she could wear in both countries without sticking out. He had American written all over him with his beat-up Nikes and T-shirt.

She could sense him walking behind her as the flight attendant scanned her boarding pass. His eyes were on her as she walked down the long corridor onto the plane. She carried her bag in front of her awkwardly as she walked down the first-class aisle and then struggled to shove it into the overhead compartment. She pushed it up repeatedly, but it kept falling down.

"You need help?" he asked her.

"Sure," she said. "Thanks."

And he tossed it up easily. Life must be a lot easier when you are a man over six feet tall, instead of a woman just over five, she thought. The world seemed to be designed for men. Life just seemed easier for men in general.

She settled down into her seat by the window. She was surprised when he took the seat next to her. He didn't look first class. Her fiancé on the other hand, he looked like he belonged in first class, she thought. He wore his dark hair short and neat, and liked to wear perfectly tailored suits to work. Tired-looking passengers streamed past them into economy, wielding bags in front of them like weapons.

"What brings you to Delhi?" she asked.

"I want to see some of India before I go to Mumbai," he said. "I'm gonna be a Bollywood actor."

"Seriously?" she said, eying his pale skin. "You don't look like a Bollywood star."

"I'm the bad guy," he said. "You?"

"I'm getting married," she said, looking out the window at the small, red lights on the ground. She wondered when the plane would take off.

"Love marriage?" he asked. "Or arranged?"

"Love marriage," she said, raising her eyebrows in response to the question. "You've been to India before, haven't you?" He sounded just like one of her relatives. It was a surprisingly common question in India, freely asked.

He nodded and she looked out the window. She felt the engine rev up and hum, then the plane began to taxi. She gripped the armrests. Her stomach still did a little somersault whenever a plane took off. She felt foolish. She had been traveling between the States and India her whole life.

She wrapped an extra blanket around her feet, pulled another one up to her neck, and shut the window. All she could see was blackness and the blinking lights on the airplane wing behind them, anyway. The windows on planes always reminded her of eyes, with heavy lids in various stages of slumber.

"Do you have cold feet, about getting married?" he asked, with a smirk and a glance down at her covered toes.

"No. My parents have been on my case for years. And he's the right guy. I'm at that age when I kind of have to get married anyway."

"You don't have to do anything," he said.

"The rules are different in India," she said. "It's all about family and honor."

"You should make your own rules," he said.

"I like those rules," she said. She clutched her bangle and ran her thumb over the pattern etched into the metal. It was something she did when she was nervous. "They come with a beautiful history and tradition."

The flight attendant walked by in her tight, navy blue skirt and leaned in. "Champagne?" she asked.

"Sure," they both said simultaneously, and she handed them their plastic flutes.

"Here's to your wedding." He raised his glass in her direction.

"Cheers," she said, taking a swig. The fizz from the bubbles tickled the tip of her nose.

She looked around and noticed there weren't many other people in first class. An old auntie wearing a pretty purple sari, white socks and sandals had been escorted out of first class for improper footwear. It didn't seem fair considering the muddy tennis shoes the American was wearing.

"You know, first class is pretty sparse. You could move to a different row, if you want more room," she said.

"I like sitting by a beautiful woman. Don't worry. I don't mean anything weird by it. I won't be a bother." He pulled out a book from his worn-out backpack.

"You know, in India I'm not considered beautiful," she said. "I'm too dark."

"Maybe you're moving to the wrong country," he said.

"I love India!" she said defensively.

"I'm not trying to offend you," he said. "I do, too. Just saying. You're the most beautiful woman I've ever seen."

"Thank you," she said. It made her sad. She shifted in her seat and pulled the entertainment console out from the armrest. She knew she should probably change seats herself, but she didn't really want to.

She flipped through the movies and started to watch one she'd seen before. She put on the airplane headphones, the cheap black foam pressed against her ears. Nothing was appealing. The picture was grainy and kept flickering in and out. She shifted in her wide seat, and the leather creaked loudly. So much for first-class luxury, she thought. She had wanted to fly first class since she was a little girl. It was kind of a letdown on the other side of the mysterious closed curtain.

She tried not to look at the man sitting next to her, now sipping a glass of scotch. He did look like the movie star type. He definitely hit the gym. In fact he smelled like the gym mingled with too much aftershave. She wondered what it would be like to give him a bath, to wash his exotic, blond hair and touch his wet, pale skin. And then she regretted the thought. What would her fiancé think? Did he think of other women all the time anyway when she was gone?

As he was reading his book, his boarding pass slipped from the pages onto the ground. She picked it up and noticed he was in the wrong seat all together. He belonged in economy.

"Why are you sitting here?" she asked, waving his ticket.

"Have you been plotting to pick me up the whole time? Were you hoping to join the mile-high club?" The moment the words came out of her mouth, she regretted them. It was not the kind of thing you want to say to a stranger, she thought.

"Well, aren't you a little freak," he laughed. "Are you blushing?"

"Brown girls don't blush," she said and swatted him with his boarding pass. She did her best to glare at him, but she couldn't help but laugh.

"Are you going to make me move?" he asked.

"I don't know," she said. "It's a long, boring flight. You're kind of interesting. Maybe I'll let you stay. It depends. Can you get me Shah Rukh Khan's autograph?"

"I'll do my best," he said. "But how will I give it to you?"

She handed him her business card. "The name's gonna change soon, though. I'll be Mrs. Malhotra."

He handed her his card and she shoved it into her pocket without looking at it.

"What's your book about?" she asked, peering at the cover.

"A photographer who has an affair with a woman while her husband's off to war. Do you think you could love more than one person at the same time?" he asked. He held the open book against his chest.

"That's such an American question to ask," she said. "No, I don't think so."

"Are you sure?" he asked. "I bet you could. I'll bet you a hundred rupees." He pulled out a squashed note from his jeans pocket and waved it in the air.

"You shouldn't crumple these," she said. "And anyway, it's not much money, you know."

"It doesn't matter. You keep it for now, so you don't forget."

"No. I'm going to sleep now," she said. "This is the silliest conversation I've ever had on a plane. You can't belong to two people at the same time."

"A woman doesn't belong to anybody," he said.

She sighed and pulled out her own headphones from her purse so she could listen to music on her phone, but the headphones were tied in knots. Her fingers struggled to untangle the white wires, and she gave up on the idea. "You like to shoot off your mouth, don't you?" she said.

"What does it matter?" he asked. "I'll probably never see you again. I can say anything I want. So can you…"

"So you're saying the rules don't apply on a plane?" she said.

"When it's international, it's duty-free," he said, smiling.

"Men are so naïve," she said. "That's not how the world works."

"Just think about it, though. You can love more than one country at a time, can't you? I bet you can. Why couldn't you love two people?"

"You can't be in two places at once." She looked him in the eye.

"Yes, you can," he said. "Okay, what if your husband died and you fell in love with another man, wouldn't you still love the memory of the first?"

"But he'd be dead."

"You can love a dead man, can't you?"

"Not literally," she said with a smirk.

She turned in her seat, pulled out the Skymall catalog and pretended to leaf through the strange and useless inventions. She stared at the stone zombie hands coming out of a pile of dirt.

"Classy," he laughed looking over her shoulder. "I don't think you can choose who you love," he said softly.

"Of course you can," she said. "Millions of people do it every-day. They enter into an arranged marriage with open hearts and open minds and many of them love each other, become best friends."

"But is that true love?" He was staring at her.

"You Americans like to chase fairy tales," she said. "You shouldn't chase happiness all your life. It's selfish. Think about the divorce rate."

"What's wrong with being happy? I'm pretty sure I could make you happy." He grinned.

"No one can make another person happy," she said. "You have to make your own happiness in life."

"And India is constantly ranked as one of the happiest places to live in the world," he said with a sarcastic smile.

"That's because of the poverty," she said.

"What's worse than an impoverished soul?" he asked.

"I'm pretty sure we have you guys beat in the enlightenment department," she laughed.

He threw up his hands and laughed. She liked the sound of it. Something about it was like music.

She finally put in her tangled headphones and reclined her seat. Closing her eyes, she let her breathing slow down with the soft music. When she woke up and tasted the stale, cottony air in her mouth, she was surprised. How had she had fallen asleep next to an unfamiliar man, she wondered. She never slept on planes.

He was still sleeping. She studied the B-movie star face some more, trying to decide whether she remembered it from somewhere. Had she seen him before, in a movie or somewhere else? She took out her digital camera and snapped a photo of him like that. He looked peaceful. As soon as the camera clicked, his eyes snapped open and he grabbed her wrist. It felt like an electric shock, like a memory.

"What are you doing?" he asked.

"Got your picture so when you're famous, I can prove I met you," she said.

"You need a better picture than that," he said, leaning in and snapping one of the two of them, holding the camera out with his hand. His cheek brushed hers. The flash had lit up a small circle of light around them in the darkness.

"Now that I'm wide awake, what am I supposed to do?" he looked down at his cell phone in airplane mode and furrowed his eyebrows. "Is this in American time or the Indian time zone?"

"American time zone most likely," she said.

"Fuck it," he said, putting it back in his pocket. "I don't even want to know how many hours we have left. However, shall we pass the time?" It was adorable the way he raised his eyebrows.

She felt her stomach give a little lurch. Was it turbulence? Had the plane dropped slightly beneath her or was it something about the stranger?

"What would you do if I leaned over and kissed you?" he asked in the dark.

She wondered where the flight attendant had gone off to, if she was sleeping in her bunk somewhere. It felt like they were the only two people on the plane just then.

"I don't know," she said. "It's a purely hypothetical question, right?"

"Maybe," he said. "Maybe not."

He leaned closer to her, so close she could feel his warm breath against her face.

"Maybe I'd slap you," she whispered.

"Maybe I'd like that," he said, raising his eyebrows and laughing.

"What would you do if I kissed you?" she asked, feeling strangely bold.

"What wouldn't I do?" he said softly.

"We'll never know," she said. "Will we?" But before the words could come all the way out, before she could even finish the thought, he had pressed his lips against hers. Pressing a hand against the side of his face, she felt the stubble lining his jaw. For a moment she thought about pushing him away, but then her hand softened. She felt the warmth of his lips, tasted a trace of alcohol. She felt a fluttering in her belly, not like butterflies, no, it was more like the feeling of turbulence, too much turbulence. What was he going to do? But there was no turbulence. She had forgotten about her fiancé. It was like he didn't exist in this kiss. But then she remembered him, thought of his face, thought of his voice, what he would say, and she slowly pulled away after an eternity of a moment.

It had felt natural. She should have felt guilty. Did she feel guilty?

"I live every day like it's my last," he said.

"Do you?" she asked.

"I do," he said.

"Like a suicide bomber," she mumbled. She had said it so quietly, but the words were jarring.

"That's one thing you shouldn't say on a plane, I guess," he said, laughing.

The lights came back on.

"Upright position, please," the flight attendant said, walking by the aisle. "We're landing soon."

She moved away from him, pressed the button and her seat came back up. Something about the routine comment had embarrassed her. She swallowed uneasily as the pressure built in her ears and set off little popping noises.

When the plane's wheels touched the ground with a thump, she had a sinking feeling in her stomach. Back to the earth. They walked through the airport together for a while. When they got to Customs and Immigration, their lines were different. He was stuck in a much longer queue. He gave a little nod as she walked past.

"It was nice meeting you," she said.

"You too, Mrs. Malhotra," he said. "Wish I could've seen more of you. Forgive me, but I did love you in a past life."

She rolled her eyes and went to the baggage claim. Her fiancé waved from the carousel. She was relieved to see him and so tired after the long flight. He didn't hug her. No public displays of affection in India. But he beamed a big, handsome smile. His intense, dark brown eyes twinkled. He took her backpack and the navy blue suitcase with scratches and a torn handle, and tossed them to the driver.

"How was your flight?" he asked.

"Tiring," she said. She wasn't sure what to tell him. Well, she knew what to tell him—nothing. There was no point. Nothing had really happened, had it? She closed her eyes on the drive home and tried to ignore the trucks and motorcycles swerving into their lane. That uneasy feeling in her stomach, the feeling of turbulence remained.

Back at their flat, she unpacked her bags and noticed the book and the 100-rupee note were in the front pocket of her carryon. The B-movie star must have put it in there when she was sleeping. Maybe it was an accident after a few too many drinks, she told herself. She sat on the bed next to her laid out gold-embroidered red wedding dress and stared at the thin, worn paper of the rupee note in her hands. Then she crumpled it some more between her fingers and her palm, just like an American.

She tried not to think of the American from the plane. He had made no promises. But his face flickered in her head for the next three days, while the henna was being applied to her hands, while she took the seven steps around the fire, and while the garland of marigolds was placed around her neck. She was in two places at once. The ground felt shaky, uneven underneath her.

After she returned from her honeymoon in Shimla, she got her photos printed and the first picture on top of the pile was the two of them on the plane. He was white as a ghost next to her dark skin, like a halo.

She knew she should've thrown it away, but she hid the photograph in the bottom of her jewelry box, along with his crumpled business card. She dropped his book and the 100-rupee note inside a manila envelope. She pulled a dollar and the spare change out of her wallet and held it in her hands. She turned the coins over and felt the ridged faces of the presidents and the English words. She told herself she liked what the American represented, a kind of freedom she didn't have or even necessarily want or need, but she could never love another man, another country, now. Could she? There was always the possibility, she thought, albeit a small one.

"Maybe in another life," she wrote on the dollar bill. She put it inside the envelope, sealed it, wrote out the address and told her driver to mail it for her.

Then she did her best to forget the American.

"I don't get it," he said in the dark.

"What don't you get?" she asked. She rubbed her hands together trying to generate some heat in her extremities. The chill was starting to set in. She shifted back into the driver's seat and turned the car back on. It was in the red zone and a huff of cold air blasted through the vents. It would take a while to warm up again.

"So she keeps his picture, but she never sees him again." His breath rose in the air, a mist around them.

"Yeah," she said.

"She seems a bit repressed."

"No, she's just an honorable woman doing what she's supposed to do," she bristled slightly. "But a woman can still have feelings. She's free to feel."

"You sound like you should be getting a Ph.D. in English lit," he said, with a laugh. "You need to drop the accounting, the M.B.A. It's not you."

She leaned closer to him on the passenger side, close enough to feel the heat through the layers on her right side, feel the heat of his breath in the small, cold space. She found herself moving closer against him as she fought the cold.

"I can still change my mind," she said. "But I have to have a day job, don't I? Out in the real world?"

"Haven't you ever heard that expression, love what you do and never work a day in your life?" he said.

"Of course," she said. "But you can also love what you do and never get work a day in your life."

"So she loves him?" he asked, raising an eyebrow.

"Maybe," she said. "I don't know. I guess that's unclear isn't it? Why not, though? Isn't it possible?"

"It's impossible to love someone that fast," he said. He furrowed his eyebrows.

"Haven't you ever met anyone that made an impression on you in a short period of time? You only spend a short, little period of time, a few hours or a few days with them, but they change the course of your life. Or you fall just a little in love and the time seems longer than it is. A week feels like a lifetime. You could get lost remembering each moment with them. Haven't you ever felt that way?"

"No," he said.

"Then you've never really been in love," she said, crossing her arms, cradling her body. She was still leaning toward him, and she was starting to feel a small ache in her back.

"Of course I have," he said, letting out a heavy breath.

"Just not that kind of love," she said.

"I think you're quite the romantic," he said. "I think the fantasy is just better than the reality. I don't think it's possible. It's impossible, impossible love." He was mumbling now. He went in and out like that. He grimaced.

"My God," she said. "You're bleeding again. Fuck. We've got to find a way to get it to stop."

She wondered if he was bleeding on the inside of his skull as well. What if he had a blood clot, and he was going to die in her arms? The panic rose inside her. She fought it down, took a gulp, took a series of deep breaths. No. She was in a kind of shock, a kind of denial. She wasn't going to think about that now.

She pressed the T-shirt bits against his head and felt the warm blood under her sticky fingers. She wished she had a way to wipe it off.

"There's got to be something in this car I can use to stop this," she thought.

She leaned over and rummaged under the seats. Her fingers danced over the grit buried there for years and found a couple of pens and an old, squashed water bottle mostly full of ice. She took a cold swig and spat it out onto the backseat because it was so stale. Her hands crinkled wrappers under the seat and touched on a fat roll of duct tape. What the heck was that doing in here, she thought.

It was from her dad. He loved duct tape. He must have left some in the car when she moved back home. He used it to seal all her boxes. It had seemed brilliant at first until it came time to unpack them. She was grateful now that it was there.

"It'll do in a bind," she said. "Maybe I should host my own survival show."

"You have to survive first," he said. "Is that sterile?" His eyes narrowed suspiciously as he glanced at the roll.

She ripped a long, gray strip of duct tape with her bare hands. "I don't think that matters so much for now." She fiddled with the bloody cotton shirt scraps.

She took a new piece of cloth and pressed it against his wound. Then she laid some duct tape over it and wrapped it around his head.

"There," she said. "How's that for pressure." He looked ridiculous, with his head bandaged like that. She would've smiled if she weren't so scared.

"It's gonna hurt like hell to take it off," he said.

"Let the hospital deal with that when you get there. At least you'll be alive. The last thing we need is you bleeding to death while we wait for help."

"I don't want to think about that," he said. "Bleeding to death. Tell me another story."

"I don't want to tell any more stories," she said. "Why don't you tell me a story? What did you study in school?"

"So now you're gonna ask me about my past lives," he said. "I'd rather not go into that right now. I'm tired."

"Oh come on," she said. "It's a simple question."

"I'm dying here," he said. "I'd rather not go into all the people I've been."

He had this weird way of not making any sense and making sense at the same time, she thought.

"Just one story," she said.

"I don't know," he said. "I guess I have a few."

"Maybe it will help keep you awake if you tell it," she said.

"I'd rather sleep… but fine. I'll tell you a story," he said. "I'm not sure you'll like it though."

"It's better than staring off into the snow," she said. Something about their situation made her think of being lost at sea, lost in a sea of snow.

It took him a few minutes to start and when the words rolled out of his mouth, he sounded like he had slipped into some kind of late-night dream. Clear but deep and dark.

"I'm not going to hold anything back," he murmured in the darkness.

CHAPTER 3
PETER'S TALE

took the water from the old well. It was a murky, yellowish brown. I tossed it out. I lifted another pail up, and it was the same. I cupped my hand and took a swig anyway. It tasted like eggs, like sulfur. I spat it out in a plume of foul-smelling mist.

I was squatting in the barn behind an old farmhouse. Its owners didn't know I was trespassing on their land. I worried they might shoot me with a shotgun if they caught me. I spotted them a few times on their way to milk the cows. They were old and gray. Mr. McGregor had a beard and glasses. The name on the mailbox was McGregor like that old kid's story about the old man and the bunny. I'm not making that up.

I had spent several nights in the old barn. I could tell it had once been grand and bright red. Now, it sagged and tilted to the right. It was almost as if the building had crooked shoulders. The wooden planks had grayed in spots like human hair. The dirt floor inside was scattered with white splotches of dried-up, caked-on bird feces. Sparrows fluttered between the beams.

At first I hesitated to unroll my sleeping bag on the filth but it was better than the bug-infested weeds outside, at least that's what I thought. Once I lay down, I counted at least a dozen nests. When I woke up in the morning, I could see the gaps and holes in the rafters, the light shining through beautiful and yellow, high-lighting the specks of dust floating through each beam.

I got up, and I went to the garden. I pulled out carrots and wiped off the dry, black clumps of dirt. I grabbed some cucumbers, too. I walked back to the old well and rinsed off the vegetables with the briny water. Small hair-like roots clung to the unpeeled carrots as I crunched through them. Then I ate a cucumber and my stomach growled.

"Did you get enough to eat?" the gray-haired woman said softly behind me. There was not a mean note to the words.

I turned and looked and dropped the vegetables on the ground. The cucumbers rolled and bumped her tennis shoe.

"Son, you could've just asked us for help," she said.

"I don't need your help," I said.

"Sometimes people like to help," she said, tucking a stray wisp of gray hair behind her ear. "It's the Christian thing to do."

"I'm not Christian," I said.

"It doesn't matter," she said. "Why are you out here?"

She reminded me of my grandmother. Her hair was held back in a loose bun. I had been stealing vegetables from a grandmother, I thought, with shame.

"I lost my job," I said. "If I'm going to be homeless, I figured it'd be better to be outside in a warmer climate, so I'm heading south."

"We could use some help, if you want a job," Mrs. McGregor said. "Come inside. I'll make you some chamomile tea."

The house had gray carpets and knickknacks of farm animals scattered on all the shelves. I took off my shoes and followed the plump, old lady into the kitchen and watched her drape an apron across her thick middle.

"I'm going to fatten you up," she said, tying her apron on with a large bow behind her. "I couldn't stand to watch you eating those vegetables out there, so skinny." She gestured out the window. "I could see you the whole time. Bacon and eggs, sound good?

"Yes, thank you," I said.

She laid out the strips of bacon on the skillet. The meat sizzled and grease splattered. I licked my lips.

"Does your husband know you're helping me out?" I said. For some reason, I felt like Mr. McGregor was going to come home and shoot me in outrage at any moment.

She scrambled the eggs and puttered a bit in response. "What I say goes in this house," she said, holding up her spatula to accentuate her point. "Don't you mind him. He's all right. He knows about you."

"Oh, he does, does he?"

"We've been wondering about you for a while," she said. "So what's your story, anyway?"

"Why do you want to know? So you can print it up in the church newsletter and tell everyone how you helped the homeless man? I don't have a story."

"Every human being has a story," she said. "You don't have to share it if you don't want to, I guess." She looked away uneasily. "What is your name though?" Mrs. McGregor asked.

"Peter," I told her. She didn't seem to catch the irony. If she did, she ignored it.

"How about your clothes," she said cheerfully. "Why don't you borrow Mr. McGregor's while I wash yours?"

She went into the bedroom and came out with a pair of coveralls and a dingy white T-shirt. "I think his regular pants would be too small for you. You can take a shower if you like, over here." She pointed to a closed door with a cross-stitch hanging from a single nail. "Here's a fresh towel. Leave your clothes out and I'll wash them."

"You're too kind," I said. I walked into the bathroom holding the clean towel. It had been two weeks since I bathed last and the grime showed in the crevices of my face, dark around the eyes and back of the neck. I still smelled of well water and bird shit.

It's amazing how stress can age a man, I thought, leaning against the old, porcelain sink and looking into the oval mirror. I looked more than forty with a light brown beard streaked with a few wisps of silver hanging from a gaunt face. I had taken off my old jacket with the brass buttons and hung it on the doorknob outside the bathroom. It was the last vestiges of my corporate life.

I had been working at the bank for eight years. I never did get into the politics of it, so I stayed at the same desk the whole time, worked in the same gray cubicle. One day, I started noticing a strange, little error no one else seemed to catch. There was some funny business with the foreign currency. It didn't matter if I was dealing in euros, crowns, pounds, or pesos, the decimal points seemed to be jumping around into the wrong places.

The customers never seemed to notice the difference. In this day and age, people seem to ignore numbers. I did have one old lady frown once when I handed her a twenty-dollar bill in exchange for a pile of pesos. She was looking at Andrew Jackson.

"The man was a murderer. The Trail of Tears," she said, "And he's on the twenty dollar bill."

Politics and banking go hand in hand apparently.

"Only twenty dollars," I muttered. It didn't seem right so I took a step back from the counter and I went back to my cubicle to look over the receipts for this transaction and another. Then I went to the envelopes where we kept the foreign cash and counted it. I know I shouldn't have unsealed it, but I had to know what was going on. I opened the envelopes and the coins and bills fell out, spilling onto my desk. It was strange. The receipts didn't match. I unsealed more envelopes, dozens of them. I went over the calculations in my head all day but the numbers didn't add up. I couldn't get the numbers out of my head. So I went to my manager, and I told him what I'd found. I placed the receipts on his desk.

"There's a problem with our foreign currency exchanges," I said. "The conversion numbers are all wrong."

"There must be a glitch with the computer system," Douglas said. "I'll check the numbers, and if it's wrong, I'll make sure this gets corrected right away."

He was swiveling back and forth on his leather chair and had his fingers interlaced in front of him.

"The numbers are wrong," I said. "I'm sure of it."

He put his reading glasses on and was leafing through the paper receipts I gave him, frowning. I turned to leave him alone in his office.

"Peter, wait," he said. "Good job catching this, thanks for bringing it to my attention. You can take the rest of the day off. You've earned it."

Now, I wasn't expecting a promotion or anything but the next day I came to work and the cops were waiting for me by the employee entrance. I didn't even get to clean out my desk. There is a picture of my old pet cat still probably hanging in a cubicle in Capital Third. They took me to the police station, gave me some bad coffee, and badgered me for hours about the whole thing, while I just stared at the brick walls and flaking orange paint.

"Your boss suspects you of stealing," the blond cop said. He had a face that was perpetually red with a long scar snaking down the side of one cheek. I wondered if someone had cut him. That's what it looked like.

"He spotted you on the video leafing through the foreign currency envelopes. Why did you open that envelope?" the cop said, pausing the video that he was playing on an old outdated monitor.

"Because there was a discrepancy," I said slowly and a little too loud. "The money the customers were giving us was not the same amount as the money headed to the main office. Some of it was missing and I showed this to Douglas. I showed it to him. I'm the one who gave him the receipts to look at, the copies didn't match, dammit!"

"Don't raise your voice at us," the officer said. "How much was it every month, a couple hundred? A grand? Was it worth it, buddy?"

"Fuck you," I said, standing up. "I didn't steal anything."

"Sit the fuck back down," the cop said, and I complied.

I rubbed my eyes like a tired child. "Why don't you ask Douglas, maybe he had something to do with it?" And then it sunk in. "Douglas must have been the one pocketing the cash."

"Sure buddy, blame the guy who caught the problem, like we haven't heard that ploy before," the cop said. "But we'll look into it."

I had handcuffs on and the metal irritated my wrists. I fiddled with them back and forth, round and round until my skin was raw. They warned me charges could be pending, but they took them off and let me go anyway.

"Don't go anywhere," they said. "Stay in town."

I took the bus home from the station. I was so angry. I was so angry I walked in the door and started packing a bag with socks, trail mix, underwear, a clean shirt, my sleeping bag. I was like a little kid running away from home with seven dollars in his pocket. I knew it was foolish, childish, stupid, but I didn't care.

All I could think was I had to get out. I had to escape. I had spent enough of my life under fluorescent lights sitting in a cubicle, with my hands tapping at a keyboard, rubbing my eyes in front of a computer screen, and I wasn't about to spend the rest of it in a jail, gripping metal bars and eating when they told me to eat. I wanted to sleep under stars.

"Don't go anywhere," echoed in my head and I said, "Fuck that," out loud. I just wanted to be free, so I started walking. That was all I wanted to do, one foot in front of the other, outside my door, down the stairs, into the woods, along the highway, the grass snaking past my ankles up to my shins.

Should I take a photo with me, one of Elizabeth? No, I wasn't going to take her picture with me. She had left me five months before, and you don't go around carrying pictures of women who leave you, not in your baggage, at least not literally. I crumpled the photo and shoved it in my pocket. I'd throw it away later.

Where to? South? To anywhere, I didn't care. I just wanted to get the hell out of there, and the funny thing was I couldn't stop thinking about the numbers. They were just bouncing around my head, the decimal points, the way they blinked on the screen. Over and over again I was doing the conversions in my head, and I couldn't get it to add up. I just couldn't let it go.

I don't know if they charged me with a crime. I don't care. I didn't commit one. It was just a mistake. I shouldn't have opened those envelopes. Was it really any of my business? I should have kept my mouth shut, maybe. No good deed goes unpunished, I thought.

The bar of soap in the shower left my skin feeling dry and sticky. I slathered it all over every crevice I could find, behind my ears, between my toes. It felt good to be clean again. I stepped out of the shower and dried myself with the fluffy towel.

I slipped on the coveralls and the white T-shirt. I looked like a young version of Mr. McGregor. I nervously popped my head outside the door and came out looking like an old-timey farm hand. It just wasn't who I was.

"Well, that's much better," she said.

We sat back down at the Formica kitchen table.

"So Peter, what are we going to do with you?" she said. "What can we do?"

"I'm no good at menial labor," I said. I'd never ride a tractor.

"You don't have to be good at it. You just have to do it."

"That's not exactly what my degree was in," I said.

"We don't care if you have a degree or not." There was something pure about the way she spoke.

"I'm a city boy, not a farm boy," I said.

"Can't you be both?" she said. "You got to let go of your pride, son."

I shook my head. "I've given up enough of my pride already." I was never going to pick up that garden hoe. I'd die first. Working with my hands seemed beneath me at the time. I was meant to work with my brain, I thought.

"Well, what's your problem?" she asked, leaning back in her wooden chair. "Tell me so I can help."

"If you were punished for something you never did and lost

everything, what would you do? Would you do it then to settle the score?"

"That depends on what it was."

Stealing, I thought. Stealing.

"Peter, you have to be more specific. How can we help you?" she said.

"I need a new profession," I mumbled. I looked away from her for a moment and stared at the large, pink flowers on the wall-paper behind her.

"You could give me your truck," I said, eyeing the key rack. "I need a ride down south."

She shook her head. "I'm not going to just give you my truck."

"I could take it," I said. "You wouldn't be able to stop me. Or would you rather give me a ride?"

"A ride?" she squeaked. "With a stranger down south? I don't think so. I'm not a country bumpkin."

I jumped up and took the keys off the key rack. I sprung through the back metal door and it swung back with a heavy slap. I ran to the old Ford truck at the start of the gravel driveway. It was unlocked and I jumped in. I started it up and flew down the driveway, with the truck kicking up the dust.

"Peter, stop!" she yelled. "Peter! Stop, thief!"

Mr. McGregor had come back from the fields. As I made my way back to the county road, I heard a shotgun ring out behind me.

I wiped my hand on the coveralls and swore. I had lost my brass-buttoned coat. What would my mother say?

But I couldn't steal from the old lady. I got about fifty miles, and I pulled over off onto a country road, the gravel spitting up from the tires, a cloud of dust behind me. I put my head against the steering wheel and thought about what I'd done. What was the point? Now I'd really be in trouble with the law. I was really in the wrong, and I'd hurt someone who showed me a kindness.

My stomach ached from the vegetables. I felt ill. The humid heat from outside the truck crept in. It was just like me to steal a truck with no AC on my way to Alabama. But somehow I fell asleep anyway. I closed my eyes and fell asleep and dreamt of children's stories, the old lady that lived in the shoe, the witch from Hansel and Gretel, and I wondered what they must have felt like, to have so many children and nothing to feed them or to have someone come and eat part of your home, call you a witch and shove you into an oven. I woke up dreaming about frosting and gingerbread, and I decided something stupid, I decided I had to go back to the nice old lady in the country house, apologize, give her back her truck. After all, she was only trying to help, wasn't she?

When I opened my eyes, the stars were twinkling, the frogs were croaking in chorus, the crickets played their own matching symphony and the last of the fireflies were flashing their light show. Take the truck back, I told myself. You aren't a thief. And so I drove back to the house. The windows were dark. I wondered where they were. I stopped the truck about 100 yards from the house, turned off the lights before I got there so they wouldn't see me.

I saw a scarecrow by the pond wearing my jacket, and remembered I was still wearing Mr. McGregor's clothes. I took off the overalls and the gray white shirt with holes under the armpits, and I pulled off my old pants and my old collared shirt and the jacket with the brass buttons from the scarecrow. I could feel straw itch against my neck, and I scratched the itch now and then as I got back into my old clothes. The old lady had a twisted sense of humor hanging my clothes up like that.

A cat was watching me on the other side of the pond. I caught the movement in the corner of my eye, the tail twitching and felt suddenly I was not alone. I froze for a moment like a small animal caught in fight or flight, unsure which strategy would save it from an owl, if anything could. And then I heard the shotgun cock behind me.

"I don't care. You can shoot," I said loudly. "I've already been shot at once today."

"But that was by Mr. McGregor," Mrs. McGregor said. "Unlike him, I don't miss."

"Look, I'm sorry, Ma'am," I said. "I'm real sorry."

"You best be on your way, son," she said. "Start walking now."

"Look, I'm sorry," I said. "I changed my mind. I felt so ashamed after you showed me how kind and Christian you were."

"I changed my mind, too, after you stole my truck," she said. "About how kind and Christian I am."

I could hear the anger in her voice, and I took a step backwards, falling into the pond. I flailed my arms in the air, but it was too late. She thought I was coming at her, and she took a shot. No good deed goes unpunished, I thought. No good deed goes unpunished.

Just like she promised, she didn't miss.

She lingered in the silence, unsure of what to say or how to feel. There was nothing but darkness in the car. Something about the story unsettled her. It had rattled off his tongue in the dark as if every detail were true. There was a familiarity to it.

"What's your name?" she asked. "You never did tell me your name."

"Peter," he said, smiling.

"Whoa," she said. "That's all made up, right?"

"I'm not dead, am I?" he said quietly with his eyes downcast.

"But that bit about the bank," she said, the panic rising in her stomach. What kind of man had she let in her car? Was he some kind of criminal? A thief?

"I'm tired," he said. "I think I need to rest for a while."

"And that bit about wandering around on the farm," she said.

"It sounded like you've been there." Was he a criminal? She wondered.

"A lot of things sound real," he said. "That doesn't mean they are. It's a fairy tale. You should know that these things aren't real. Aren't you a writer?"

"But Peter," she said. "You're not a writer. At least you never said you were."

"Maybe I'm just a storyteller." He smiled again. Or was it a grimace? "It's a modern spin on The Tale of Peter Rabbit for Christ's sake. Didn't your mother ever tell you any stories when you were a kid?" He laughed.

You are the most cheerful dying hitchhiker I've ever met, she thought. The bandage was dark crimson in the back. How could he be so articulate and be dying at the same time? Maybe he was playing up the injury, she thought, no, she felt kind of ashamed for thinking that. He couldn't fake that amount of blood.

"How can you be so good at telling stories after a blow to the head?" she asked him. Everything seemed suspicious, his whole story.

"It's one of the great mysteries of the universe," he said. Then he blinked a few times and closed his eyes.

Peter's head rolled forward. Fuck, she thought, he was passing out. No he wasn't passing out. She stared at him, a muffled panic building up inside her.

He stirred. His eyes blinked open.

"What?" he asked. "I was just sleeping."

"I'm not so sure about that," she said.

She handed him the bottle of stale water and told him to drink it. After all, it couldn't really hurt anything. He gulped it down and wiped his mouth with his sleeve.

"Peter," she said. "I think I should leave the car and try to get some help. I don't think anyone can see us where the car is with all the snow. Can I borrow your boots?"

Why hadn't she thought of it before?

"Over my dead body," he said. "Don't you remember what

you said about the survival shows? They always say to stay with the car. I feel much better after the water. Much better."

"Okay," she said.

"What's your name?" he asked softly. "You never told me your name. Where are your manners, my friend?"

"Julie," she said.

"Julie," he murmured. "What does it mean? Ahhh." He closed his eyes and opened them again. "It means young. You are a young soul. And I'm an old, troubled soul."

His answer sent chills down her spine. He was right. How did he just know the meaning right off the top of his head like that?

"Why don't you tell me something about yourself?" she asked. "Why don't you tell me about Elizabeth?"

"What's there to tell?" Peter said.

"What's she like?" Julie asked. "Is she real?"

"Yeah, Elizabeth is real," Peter said. "She's very beautiful, too beautiful for her own good. She was given everything, because of it. Everyone always said she was spoiled. But I didn't listen. I loved her anyway.

"I remember the first time I took her on a date. I remember the earrings she wore, pieces of sparkling glass and dangling metal. She drank just a little too much. I remember her slurring her words ever so slightly, nodding forward with those earrings bobbing below her ears. But there was something magnetic about her. She could always make me smile. She knew how to look at a man.

"I carried her home. She was wearing shoes, stilettos, and they weren't comfortable and she kept complaining about them so I flipped her over my shoulder with her legs dangling in front of me, one hand on her calf, trying not to impale my hands on her damn shoes. I carried her back to her apartment, and I put her to bed. I remember her putting her arms around my neck as I leaned over her, begging me to stay. So I did, and I never really left. We moved in together a couple months later. I don't think she liked to be alone, said she spent too much time alone as a kid. Well, that's what her therapist told her anyway."

Julie nodded but didn't say anything.

"I was always disappointing her," Peter said. "We fought over the credit card bills. I'd tell her she was spending too much on clothes, that we didn't make enough money for designer labels, that I couldn't keep paying the rent alone. I was trying to save. She never yelled, said she didn't want to be like her parents, but she had this silent streak. She could hurt you with her silence, could wield it like a weapon for days.

"'What are you saving for?' she'd finally say. 'I don't want a house. We don't have kids. Let's just live a little.'

"'But I want a house, I want kids, well one day, and that's not going to happen with a lousy credit score,' I told her."

"'You don't understand what it's like to be a woman,' Elizabeth said. 'We have to keep up appearances.'

"I remember the way she uttered those words, with a glare and a glance that said, my appearance, well, it left something to be desired. I had put on a few pounds then. This was before I started hitting the gym."

Julie tried to imagine Peter's face rounded out with a little weight. His jaw was a harsh line in the dark. "But surely there must have been a reason you loved her," she said, searching his face. "Was it just because she was beautiful?"

"No," Peter said. "I think it was because she needed me. We needed each other. She could be so sweet at times. Or maybe it was more primal than that, a physical reaction, a chemical reaction that I just couldn't help. Do you get to choose who you love? What if they aren't worthy of your love? Do you get to choose then?"

"I bet you would have spoken more highly of her before your breakup," Julie said.

"Yeah, probably," Peter said, shrugging his shoulders. "You know, my heartbreak is really none of your business."

There was an awkward silence broken by the sounds of the

car. One last cough of hot air spurted out of the vents as the engine shuddered. Julie let it shudder a few times before she turned the key to the off position. She didn't want to total the car over one last puff of warmth. He looked at her, and she looked at him, and she knew it was just a matter of time before she was back in his lap again with his hot breath on her face and the blood trickling down onto her jacket, too.

"Crawl back over here," he said, motioning with his pointer finger at her. "I'm cold."

And she did crawl over there because what else was she going to do? It was a question of survival.

They were face-to-face and she got to see the little lines on his face, around his eyes and mouth, the dots of his pores, and breathe in his scent. He didn't smell like a homeless man. He smelled like he had showered recently. She could smell soap on his skin, also another smell, that human smell. He didn't smell homeless. What a strange, little shallow thought.

"I don't want to be here," Peter said, breathlessly. "I want to be anywhere but here. Can't you just take my mind off of all this? Take me on another trip. Take me anywhere but here and this shitty car. Tell me a story about the currency of love. Tell me a story about a boy and a girl who actually love each other."

"That's a tall order," Julie said, furrowing her eyebrows. "I'm worried I'm going to put you to sleep."

"That's okay," he said. "Consider it a lullaby, a bedtime story."

"But I'm afraid of you going to sleep. You might not wake up."

"I'll stay awake," he said. "Besides, these stories, passing stories to pass the time, it was your idea anyway. What else are we going to do?" He raised an eyebrow.

CHAPTER 4
THE DANISH SUN

The Danish sun was dimming, but the sky was streaked in red and violet hues. The two of them sat on the bench and watched the evening and morning blend together. They watched the brief, precious darkness and then the first yellow streaks of sun glow through it.

"I can't remember if it's dawn or evening," he said.

"Is there a difference?" she said, laughing.

The bench overlooked a green pond. It snapped into focus bathed with the bright light. Two ducks swam by. The day had begun in the night.

"I love the Danish sun in summer," he said. "It never seems to end."

She smoked a cigarette while they sat there. All the Danish girls smoked, well almost all of them. The smoke hung heavy and gray around them.

"I don't ever want to leave," she said quietly. "I love this place."

The words made him swallow. He had asked her what she thought of living in the States, but he told himself it didn't matter right now. It was too beautiful of a nighttime dawn to worry about such things.

She had her legs stretched out in front of her and his hand was on her thigh. The white dress had ridden up a bit, a distraction. He wondered if she did it on purpose or if she had just had that many drinks.

They had stumbled out of the club, sweaty and tangled hours ago. The pulsating music had crushed them together, dancing in a kind of collision. It was almost pitch black in the place aside from the strobe lights flashing. He had Carlsberg after Carlsberg and danced with the green bottle in his hand. But the buzz was wearing off. The beauty was wearing off. The day was starting at night.

The reality was breaking through the dawn, red and bloody like broken sunlight. She wasn't coming to the States. And he wasn't moving here.

"Don't you love me?" he asked.

She sighed. "Of course, I do."

"But you say you'll never leave Denmark."

"Honey, a relationship is based on compromise," she said.

"Then compromise," he said.

Her face turned ashen. The rosy cheeks drained of all their colors.

"Why should I be the one to compromise?" she said. She smirked as she said it, but he could see the corners of her eyes pinch into a glare.

He had broken the rules. She had explained them to him from the start. You don't boss a Dane around, and you don't act arrogant. He had done both. Would she still love him?

Like an answer, she interlaced her fingers in his. He stared at their hands together, pale and bathed in the bright four a.m. sun.

"We have months to figure it out," he said.

"Months for me to convince you to stay," she said smugly. "I have my methods, mister." She rubbed his leg gently.

No one else was in the park, near the pond. The whole place was deserted aside from the ducks. The shiny green head of the mallard caught his eye.

"Long distance is a killer. I'm not doing long distance," she said simply.

It was like they had entered contract negotiations, he thought. It wasn't so simple. There were restrictions. He was there as a student not a permanent resident. Would the government even allow him to work there, to stay? And what about her in the United States? Which country would welcome them with open arms, if either would?

"How do you choose between two countries?" he asked.

"I don't know," she said. "How do you choose between two families? Two sets of friends?"

She leaned her head against his shoulder. He could smell the shampoo. The reddish blond tendrils glowed in the light, like copper mixed with gold.

"You are my family," he said. "You are my friend. Do we need anyone else? Why do you have to give me an ultimatum?"

He wished he could stay drenched in the Danish sun with her holding his arm forever. They walked around the pond for a while. The green water shone brightly, specks of white flashing on its surface.

"Haven't you ever belonged to a place?" she said. She stopped to hold the rail. She leaned her stomach against it. The white dress fluttered behind her in a soft wind.

"Maybe I belong to you," he said. "But I don't belong to a place.

"What about the winter?" he added. "The darkness."

"There's no darkness with you," she said. "Was it so bad last winter? We'll light candles."

They had been in the darkness under the streetlights. The two of them had met under a thin coating of ice and drizzle, waiting for the bus in the black. In a city where no one looked you in the eye, she had been so friendly. It hadn't been so bad last winter, he thought, drinking wine and burrowing under a down comforter that floated above them like a cloud.

It was hard to remember that darkness now that there was so

much sun. The pond was glittering under its rays. They walked to her studio and she fumbled with her keys. They stood in an empty hallway surrounded by white walls.

"Here we are," she said.

She swung open the door and the room was drenched in white. The curtains were still up. It still felt like day at night. Her photos hung across the ceiling from a crisscross of wire. Some were black and white. Some were color. She was the best photographer he had ever met.

He hadn't seen these shots yet. She was the only one he knew who still printed out her photos and displayed them. There were a hundred of him hanging overhead. Their whole six-month history hung in midair. There he was walking next to the water, laughing and looking down. There he was sleeping, with his black hair crushed against the white pillow.

There they were dancing and drinking wine. There he was walking through Tivoli Gardens, smelling the pink roses, with their shadows streaking the winding sidewalks. There he was cooking in the white kitchen, shirtless with a spatula in his hand. In another one, she had flour on her nose. He took that shot. Then the weekend vacation she had taken him on. There was a picture of him standing victoriously on the top of a giant sand dune, like he'd climbed Everest, looking out at the sea. Photos of them painting the apartment together, the light blue streak she swiped across his cheek. It took a lot of scrubbing to get that off. The paint was in his hair for weeks.

There was a photo of the tip of Jutland with the sand jutting out and the waves crashing together, where the North Sea and Baltic Sea come together. He pulled it off the wire and stared at it, the choppy dark blue waves smashing and glittering under the sun and crashing against the light blue ones, battering the jagged line like a bad border. They had gone swimming there. She had changed on the beach like her nakedness was nothing. Was he in the picture? He wondered.

"Two seas colliding," she said, looking over his shoulder, her hot, minty breath on his neck. She'd been brushing her teeth.

"I know," he said. "It's choppy."

"Just like us," she said with a smile.

"How are we going to figure this out?" he asked.

"A fight to the death," she waved her toothbrush like a sword. "Is that the right expression?"

"Rock paper scissors?" he joked.

"What's that?" she smiled.

"Never mind," he said. "I'd have an unfair advantage. Years of practice. We could move to neutral territory. How about Switzerland?"

She laughed. "How about a coin toss?"

She rummaged through her purse and handed him a Danish crown. It seemed like such a great idea at four a.m. He didn't normally make decisions in the middle of the night but it looked like midday out the window.

"Tails for Denmark," she said.

"Is this legally binding?" he asked.

She nodded. He flipped the coin high in the air, caught it and slapped it against his wrist. There she was, the queen, looking at him. He cupped his hand over the coin. He looked up at her. Half her face was covered in sunlight, drenched in it by the open window. Her hair had caught the rays of fire. One wide eye was a light blue, the other steely blue in shadow. Her mouth was pointed in an O.

"What is it?" she said.

Heads or tails, a declaration of love, he thought. He couldn't do it to her.

"Tails," he said. "Best two out of three?"

"No way," she said.

"We have a lot to think about," he said. "It's just a coin, you know."

"I know," she said.

They crawled into bed. She inched up close to him, her head

under his chin, her breath on his neck, her heartbeat crushed against his heart, like two pounding tides. They were like two seas rolling and crashing together, black and blue and shimmering under the Danish sun.

"They are gambling again," Peter laughed. "They made a bet in your last story, too. Do all your characters gamble?"

"Sorry," she said. "It's hard to think of something original at 12:30 a.m. At least I took you somewhere warm and sunny." She shuddered from the cold. It was starting to creep into her extremities, a constant reminder of the trouble they were in.

"I like it," he said. "Isn't all love a gamble? You never know how it's going to turn out. The other person can change. In fact people have to change to stay together. You use spare change as a metaphor, don't you?"

"Maybe," she smiled. "Or maybe I don't put that much thought into things, well consciously at least. A lot of it's subliminal. I just tell the story as I imagine it. Why won't you tell me your story, your real story?"

"I'm not supposed to," he said, inhaling sharply though his nose.

"Why?" she said. "Is it classified information? Are you a secret agent?"

He laughed.

"I'm surprised you can laugh, considering how beat up you are," Julie said.

"It's part of the training," he said. "After a lifetime of pain." His features contorted. She touched his head, to feel if the blood had soaked through. The makeshift bandage seemed to be working, for now. Barely.

"How do you get through it?" She pressed herself against the warmth of his chest. She couldn't help it. The chill was seeping through the sleeping bag. So was a distant worry. What if they died out here on this deserted county road? The thought flickered in and out of her mind.

"I'm an optimist," he said. "I'm a glass half full kind of guy."

"And yet you say we are gonna die at four a.m.?"

"Yeah, it's hard to be an optimist and a psychic, I guess," he said. "You always know how it's going to end, with angels and demons and heaven and hell. Which do you like better?"

"Heaven, of course," Julie said. It was an easy answer.

"Baby, on a good day, I could take you to heaven," he said, raising his eyebrows.

"Oh please," she said, laughing and pulling back. Julie had gotten used to his smell. She had gotten used to his breath on her face. She wasn't so afraid of him in this moment, just glad he was alive. She was too tired to be afraid and fear felt pointless now anyway. And he seemed so helpless, that was the thing. Wasn't he helpless? How bad was the blow? No, she still couldn't sleep.

He had one arm around her and it was oddly comfortable, like they had known each other for years, not hours. The cold had made them close companions. She was glad she wasn't alone in the dark. She hated the dark.

"Your turn now," she said. "You tell me another one."

"Did I ever tell you I was a sailor?" he asked. "When I was young. I could tell you a story or two…"

CHAPTER 5
NO EXITS

The halyards slap slap in a whipped frenzy of wire. I pull my head under the sleeping bag and try to drown out the noise. The waves crash against the side of the hull and I can hear the gurgle of the water tanks below my bed, settee, whatever the hell you want to call that three-inch piece of foam between my stomach and the tank below. The radio goes in and out, a mixture of fuzz, beeping and the music of one vessel hailing another.

"Get up," Captain Kim calls. He has a gravelly voice that's laced with a hard liquor hangover and a touch of Australia. "The clients are going to be up any moment."

Tracy and Richard Wilson, our clients, rented the Virginia, a fifty-five-foot yacht with us as crew for their fifth anniversary. Why the hell would anyone with their kind of money want a romantic sailing expedition to Canada when they could go to the Bahamas? It's a mystery to me, but hey, I'm glad because I get a paycheck and a chance to set sail.

I can feel the sweat building under my armpits, wet and sticky under a sleeping bag perfectly rated for summer in Canada. A negative-ten degree rating might seem like a bit too much insulation, but the last icebergs were sighted halfway through June. It is by no means a tropical paradise, but it certainly does have its charms, if you don't factor in the insects the size of small birds.

Did I mention the North Shore of Lake Superior has mosquitos that suck the life out of your arms at sunset? I can hear one of them whining now, so I keep my head under the bag.

"Seriously, get the hell up."

"We've been together seven years, and you still don't know how to wake me up in the morning, honey?"

Kim chuckles. "Fuck you."

"Food," I moan, "I'll get up if you fucking feed me."

"I should really fire you," he says. "You're such a fucking princess."

"Oh come on, love. When you're at sea, you can't be so picky, you know."

"The clients might hear you," he hisses.

"So what if they do," I say. "It's a free world, Kim. People are more accepting."

"But we're not even gay," Captain Kim says.

"No, I don't think we are," I mutter as Tracy Wilson comes out of her cabin in a short bathrobe and darts into the head, the tiny compartment of a bathroom in case you didn't know.

"Look at those pipes," I say.

I scurry out of my sleeping bag, stuff it into a cubby behind the cushions and sit down at the fold-out table in the galley and eat some runny eggs Kim has set out for me on a paper plate. They taste like the frying pan, drenched in burnt butter that has solidified and congealed into ash. The yolk bursts against my tongue, and I swallow them as fast as I can so I won't have to taste them a second time.

"You burnt them on purpose, you ass," I say.

"They aren't that bad," he says.

"Don't feed that to Tracy and Richard," I say.

"They like yogurt and granola," he says.

"Well, that's fortunate," I say.

It's a good thing because the smell is nauseating as the cabin fills with a haze of smoke. Kim smells like eggs and whiskey and rum mixed with smoke and grease. I join him in the galley to help him with the dishes and feel his plump butt cheek brush against mine. I do not particularly enjoy this, but quarters are tight on the Virginia. I pick up the old sponge and it also has that scent, the scent of something that has gone bad.

Have things already started to go bad? I wonder. Tracy and Richard have been on board for a week and a half. Kim was happy to have the long-term booking, but here we are in the wilderness with two people we have nothing in common with. Two unpredictable human beings, strangers with a lot of money and a lot of expectations. Two people who regularly cuss each other out behind the teak door.

I heard him call her a bitch. I heard her call him a dumb fuck. The words were loud and muffled by the woodwork.

But then again, Kim and I regularly cuss each other out. And in our own ways, we love each other too. Who are we to judge and question the state of our clients' matrimonial affairs?

Tracy comes to the galley in the same bathrobe after her shower with her long blond hair snaking against the white terry cloth caressing her shoulders. She has porcelain skin that makes you ache to touch it. Are her legs really that smooth?

Damn, Kim and I have been doing these sorts of gigs all summer. It's a lonely life. You get paid to sail, but it's a lonely life. And there she is drinking her coffee with her long fingers wrapped around the mug, her flushed red lips pressed against it, her eyes reaching up to mine in mock surprise. How could she not know everyone is looking at her? Isn't she used to it by now? Of course she is. Isn't every rich man's wife?

She sits at the teak table, crosses her legs and dangles the top one back and forth in front of us in a bouncy motion. I try not to watch her leg move, but my pupils tend to jerk back and forth like a cat stalking its prey. When did I get so bad about discretion? This is the problem with long sails. You go back into town and no one wants to come close to you because of two things: You've lost your manners, and your clothes stink. Meanwhile, you are so desperate for conversation you've got this big, ridiculous grin on your face and a tendency to get too close. Another human being! Thank God! Now, talk to me, please, for the love of god. How many times can I talk about Sydney with Kim?

We sit at the teak table and Tracy asks us if either of us is married. I shake my head no.

"I was married," Kim says. "To the original Virginia."

"What happened?" she says with concern dripping from her soft voice.

"The second Virginia," I say. "He's really married to the boat."

"True enough," he says wiping a rag across the wooden table. "She didn't like that I was gone sailing all the time."

"Why didn't she just come with you?" Tracy asks. I wonder if paying customers feel entitled to know everything about our personal lives.

"She got seasick," Kim says.

"A lot of women get seasick," she says. "From all the ups and downs."

Is she being literal or metaphorical? Because to be honest I can't tell. I furrow my eyebrows and look at her. Sometimes I think you need a college degree to understand a woman, but then I remember I've got a college degree from a past life tucked somewhere in a drawer on land, a place from another set of seasons.

"You know there are things you can do if you are seasick," I say. "There are patches and tricks to help you through it. You just have to stare at the horizon."

"Stare at the horizon," she said. "Huh. Do you ever get seasick?"

"Only landsick," I smirk but it's true. You get used to the gentle rocking motion and then when you set foot on stationary land, it throws off your whole system.

Tracy walks into the V-berth cabin and comes out with a yellow sweater and a pair of white shorts. It's the perfect combination for the Canada North Shore, with its schizophrenic weather, and I like the fact that I can still see her legs.

"Would you take me to shore for a bit?" she says. "Richard isn't interested in coming. He wants to sleep in some more."

We climb the steps into the cockpit and I swing open a locker, bending over to pull out two orange life jackets. I hand her one. Seagulls caw overhead and the flies crawl across the white fiberglass.

"I can't quite get this," she says, and I help her untangle the black straps. She clicks the buckles.

"Get in the boat." I point down over the edge. She scampers down the ladder.

I get in the dinghy, and I pull the cord on the engine. It sputters and roars, and we get the hell away from the Virginia.

"I want to feel land," she yells over the roar.

The nose of the rubber vessel hops over the waves, smacking on top of them, the spray cascading up. And I'm grinning and smiling as I feel the moisture on my face, like morning dew. And Tracy, well, she's just holding on to the black rubber handles, her long legs splayed out, her tan leather boat shoes gripping the wooden floorboards.

I cut the engine, flip it up and the dinghy glides over the clear water, over the rocks and then I hop out and pull it to shore, over the sand, hoisting the rope up and tying it to a tree in a sheer act of paranoia. Because there isn't much of a tide on Lake Superior, but I guess it's just a habit from the other places I've sailed. But it's always good to tie things down, isn't it?

We get on shore, and I help her unbuckle her orange life vest, not that I have to, but I like being close to her, and she doesn't seem to mind. We leave our shoes in the dinghy and walk across the reddish brown sand. It's wet and cool under our bare feet.

Two children building a sandcastle stop and point excitedly at the Virginia off in the distance. I grin. I'm proud of her size.

"Wish that boat was mine, not Kim's," I mutter. "But then

again, I know the kind of sacrifices you have to make for a boat. He's poured his whole life into her."

"Would you be willing to do that for the Virginia?" she asks. "If she were yours?"

"Hell yes," I say.

It's the sails that get you, the breath of life, breath of wind pushing you forward. The feeling of floating, flying, zipping by at an angle. The whole world tilts as you feel the roar of the wind. The waves break against the bow, the Virginia's nose. They foam and curl and crush and pound. And she just keeps plowing forward.

But I know Tracy will never understand this. It's lost on her. Tracy likes to hide in the cabin below reading a book, painting her nails, trying to hold herself steady against the sway.

"It's better if you don't fight it," I had told her the day before. "It helps if you get up and look at the horizon."

She lowered her head and looked up again, her blond hair dangling down and gave me a green look.

"Here, let me show you some pressure points to push that help with seasickness," I told her. I grabbed her wrist with its soft, silky white skin and pressed my thumb between two veins in vain. This was the first time I had touched her skin.

"Push here, and it'll make you less queasy."

"Thanks," she said sheepishly. "You know, I really don't like sailing, no offense."

"None taken," I said.

But I had gone upstairs and noticed Richard was in trouble, not the kind of trouble you'd expect, the kind that comes from loving a woman who doesn't love to sail.

There he was at the helm, with his brown hair flowing behind him. There he was trimming the sail, pulling in the line, wrapping it around the metal winch and winding it in tighter. There he was at the mast, hoisting the white fluttering cloud of a sail, each fold of fabric unfurling in a white whoosh.

He had a shit-eating grin on his face and you know he meant it when he sat down in the cockpit next to Kim and said with seriousness in his eyes, "How much for the Virginia?"

"She's not for sale," Kim said. "But thanks."

Was it the first time anyone had asked to buy the boat? Yes, Kim told me later, and he didn't like it. "It's kind of like someone asking you if they can fuck your wife for the right amount of money," he said. "You get tempted and pissed off at the same time."

So Tracy and I are walking down the beach and she asks me. "Don't you ever get lonely, with all this sailing?"

"I meet people all the time," I say. "New people in every harbor, hail my friends on the radio. It's its own little world."

"I'm so bored," she says. "I get bored. I need civilization. Humanity."

She picks up a stone from the sand and fingers it before throwing it into the water. It skips two times.

"That's not how it's done," I say. "You have to pick the right stone to throw." I pick up a black one. It's smooth and flat on each side. I rub the sand off it, hook my finger around it and fling it back and forward. With eight little skips, it dances and hops across the small waves.

"I want to swim," she says simply, and she pulls off her white shorts and takes off her yellow sweater. She's left in her purple lace bra and mismatched cotton underwear as she runs into the water, a spray flying up behind her. I stare at the crumpled white denim and yellow cotton lodged in the sand with my mouth slightly open. She's shrieking from the cold and the delight and then laughing. Her blond hair has darkened into wet, winding ropes that hang across her shoulders, and now she's pulling me in. She has her fingers around my wrists, tight as handcuffs, and I can feel her pulling me in. Her thumbs are pressing on that same pressure point between the veins. Her fingers are icy and so are the icy cold fingers of Lake Superior touching my skin, the water shooting into my pores like needles as I wade in after her. My skin goes pale and slightly blue tinged under the water as it gets colder and starts to numb. That's the thing about swimming in Lake Superior. It's not so bad once your legs go numb.

There's Tracy with her lace bra soaked through, wearing cotton underwear on bottom. And she's laughing and splashing me and calling me, "Wuss."

And she's still got a wet grip on me and we do kiss, you know. I kiss her because she's beautiful, and I am lonely, and she kisses me because well, I guess I'm beautiful and lonely, and here we are two lonely, beautiful people freezing on the beach.

Her lips are cold and fish-like and I wonder if she is a mermaid for a moment, a silly, little, delirious, wet thought. My fingers get caught in the wet tangle of lavender lace. I'm like a fish caught in a net.

And the warmth spreads from my lips across my neck and chest and down my stomach but stops at the line where the icy cold water laps against my hips.

So I step back and turn to look at the Virginia, and I start to swear. I see two stick figures in the cockpit. Are they watching? Fuck. The icy cold is dripping across my shoulders, across my face, and I wipe my face with my fingers, and I wonder.

You see on a boat, there are no exits. Kim and I have talked about this a few times in the dark under the northern lights, watching out for tankers. Each passenger we bring on is a stranger. We have to do our best for smooth sailing. They come on like cardboard figures and with time we know more about them than their families in some cases. Boats are tight quarters. You learn a lot about people when you live with them on a boat. You learn what shape their hair comes out in in the morning, the names they call out during sex, the names they call each other in general, the good ones and the bad ones, you learn what they like to eat, what makes them sick, how they handle their alcohol, and how they puke.

I watched Tracy puke a few days ago. The long blond waves

swaying back and forth as she hurled into a white, plastic bucket. Richard did not hold her hair back. And so I stepped in and did it. Her chest heaved. I tried not to look at the orange and red and yellow mess. I tried not to smell the scent of stomach acid drifting up. The hair was soft and slippery in my hands, thin and golden. But I couldn't wait to let it go.

And here she is now, a wet mess, staggering back onto the red, brown sand.

"Fuck," I say. "It was only a kiss."

We are back in the dinghy and I'm rowing and rowing. The engine wouldn't start. It sputtered and choked and coughed out a diesel cloud but it would not start. And she's there, sitting behind me, next to the dead engine. I can feel her eyes watching my movements, her eyes watching my arms, my back, burning into the muscles. Or maybe I'm just imagining it because I look back and one of her long fingers is trailing in the water, creating a little stream.

We are quiet and all I can hear is the sound of the plastic oars dipping and dripping into the water, and the waves crashing and whooshing onto the beach.

Things aren't that great between you two, are they? I want to ask the question but I don't dare. I don't dare. It's just like the engine that won't start. I kill the words when they reach my lips, swallow them and just keep rowing.

I notice I'm edging away from the Virginia, and so I pick a point on the horizon and guide myself back. There's a pine tree, tall and green behind a boulder. That's the one that will get me to the Virginia. Just got to keep my eyes off Tracy.

When we get on board, the yelling starts and Richard is trashing the place. He's banging the table with his fists. He rips out a lamp from the wall. The gas lantern is thrown to the wooden floor and its glass globe shatters. He keeps calling her a bitch over and over again.

Tracy is oddly quiet, like she's been through this before and it no longer scares or shocks her, but Kim is screaming and red faced. The man is hurting his Virginia.

"Stop it," Kim yells. "Stop it!"

Richard scratches the wooden paneling with his rigging knife. He stabs a cushion and white stuffing flies out of it, like snow cascading around us.

"What the hell is wrong with you?" Kim asks. "Sadistic bastard."

"You sure you want to talk to me like that?" Richard says.

He's got the rigging knife in his hand, and he's flipping it open and shut. "It's only a two-inch blade, but it's sharp enough," he says, looking down at it.

"I didn't have you pegged as a homicidal maniac," I say. "Look, we were just playing around in the water."

"Like hell," he says, lunging toward me.

I'm not normally a fast thinker, but this time I am. I step backward and grab the flare gun out of the navigation station. I point the orange barrel at his head. He doesn't know it, but it's a bluff. The last thing I'm gonna do in the world is shoot off a flare inside the boat. It would just start the Virginia on fire. So I tack in another direction.

"Look, I have no interest in your wife. I'm not even straight," I yell, "I'm gay, for Christ's sake."

"Like hell you are," he says. But he backs down.

"Kim, for the love of god, if you know what's good for you, kiss me!"

With that, I pull Kim close to me and kiss him as passionately as I can muster. All five senses are on fire. His protests catch in my mouth. I cup his prickly round face. I pull his face close to mine.

And Richard busts out laughing and bends at the waist, letting out a rush of breath in relief.

Kim wipes his mouth after our kiss but plays along the best he can.

"Why don't you sleep in the same cabin then?" Richard asks.

"Because it would be unprofessional. It makes some of our clients uncomfortable," Kim says.

"Well, it doesn't make us uncomfortable," Richard says. "Does it, honey?"

Tracy shakes her head.

Sadistic bastard, I think.

And for the rest of the fucking trip I spend the night in Kim's cabin, with my back to him and his back to me. The body heat radiates off his body. His breath is loud and gaspy in the night. Occasionally I can feel him kick me. But I'm happy because I'm home safe. The Virginia is my home. The Virginia is safe.

Tracy and Richard, they have their door open to their little cabin. They are murmuring and cuddling, and the boat is rocking them to sleep, too. Tracy has stopped hiding below deck during the day. She has taken off the Dramamine patches and started hoisting the sails. Maybe there's some hope for them yet.

As for me and Kim?

"Maybe we should actually give this thing a try. Wink wink," I say to him first thing in the morning as we wake up peering into each other's eyes.

"Fuck you," he says. "I have only one love."

"I know. I know. The Virginia."

"I'm going to send that asshole a bill for all the damage after we get back in port," he murmurs.

I roll over and go back to sleep. The flare gun is tucked under my pillow, in its case of course.

"What do you think?" Peter said. "How's that for a sailing story?"

Julie crawled off him. "Be quiet," she said, putting a gloved finger to her lips. "I think I hear something." There was a distant whoosh and she got out of the car as fast as she could. The car door hung open behind her, letting the cold and snow drift in. She waved her arms in the dark and the car drove right on past, a flash of yellow and red lights mingled with white snow

"Mother fucker!" Julie yelled after it. "You saw me!"

"Come on!" Peter murmured. "We're dying out here."

She got back in the car and slammed the door behind her.

"I know they saw me," Julie said. "They fucking saw me, and they still didn't stop."

"I tell ya, it's a cold, cold world out there," Peter said. "Nobody was stopping for me when I was out there walking along this road."

"What the hell were you doing out here all alone, anyway?" she asked. "God, it's cold."

She climbed right back into his lap under the sleeping bag, shivering.

"I am a lost, wandering soul," Peter said quietly.

"Were you really a sailor?" she asked. She couldn't stop shaking. She had let too much cold air into the car when she had flung open the door.

"Yes," Peter said, "But the story is mostly made up. I did work with an Australian guy named Kim, but I never got around to sleeping with him."

"Did you love him?" she asked.

"God, you get personal," Peter said. "Nosy, nosy... not in that way, but I did have a thing for a girl named Tracy once."

"Hmm," Julie said. "I thought she was just a sex object."

"Maybe she started out that way," he said. "It has to start somehow."

He wrapped his arms tighter around Julie just then. She almost didn't wish she could escape.

"Do you miss Elizabeth?" Julie asked. "Did she start out as a sex object? You can tell me more about her, if you want."

"Not a lot to tell," he said, loosening his grasp. "We were together for five years."

"What happened?"

"She left me." He grimaced in the dark.

"I'm sorry to hear that," she said. "Why?"

"You're like a little bit of barbed wire, aren't you?" he murmured. "Can't you see I'm in pain?" He took a sharp intake of breath.

"Fine," she said. "I'll leave you alone."

"No," he said. "You can keep talking, talk about anything, anyone. Just keep talking. I don't want to be alone with my thoughts anymore."

Was he crying? She could see a tear forming at the edge of his eye, but maybe it was just the cold. His tears made her shudder. He wasn't going to rescue her. No one was going to rescue her. It was going to be up to her to find a way out of that car, if there was a way out. She wanted to jump, to leap out into the snow and just run away as far as she could. But they were trapped. They were in it together.

The snow was piling higher and higher around the car. It had blown up on the windows in curved white arcs.

"I've got another story I could tell you," she said, shivering. "I wrote it a long time ago. It's in first person. I hate writing in first person, because everyone always thinks it's me."

"Is it?" he said.

"No," she said. "Of course not."

CHAPTER 6
CHUCK AND IRENE

D id you know a house from the 1950s could be built on a wooden foundation in Jackson County? It was actually up to code at the time. That's what happens when you let people build their own houses. They get inventive. They get creative. And what do you get when you buy one? You get rot and a whole lot of cuss words when the inspector comes.

"I've never seen anything like this," the inspector said. "What were they thinking?" The man literally scratched his head.

Irene and Charles Taylor built this house and lived here fifty years. It's not ugly. It's not a house you would think was on the verge of collapse. It's a ranch style with a triangular overhang. It's got white vinyl siding and burgundy trim.

Outside, the children's tricycles and a plastic grocery cart are scattered on the lawn. There isn't a single creeping Charlie among the blades of grass. I'm proud of the lawn.

The porch stairs are covered in green vinyl carpeting. I admit that's ugly. Monte and I know we should take it off, but we haven't figured out what kind of adhesive Chuck and Irene used to keep it together. I'm afraid it would look even uglier if we peeled it off, so we leave it on.

But inside the house is nice and cozy. Inside, there's layer after layer of white carpeting. I like the feel of it under my bare feet.

Except for the kitchen. In the kitchen, there's a wooden floor and you can roll marble after marble across it in the same sloping arc. The children were the ones who first noticed our house was sinking. Children notice everything, you know.

I like making the kids' lunches on the linoleum counter. Peanut butter and jelly. I lick the knife and put it in the dishwasher even though I know it's never going to get clean. I don't care. I'll run it again and again with each new load of dishes. Because eventually it will come clean, right? Or someone else will clean it for me. That's the ultimate denial: peanut butter residue.

"Can we prop up the south end of the house?" I asked the inspector.

Monte wasn't even there when he came this morning.

"No, ma'am. I'm afraid not," he said. "You're gonna have to move. You're going to have to let the county condemn this place."

"Please don't tell the county," I pleaded. "We need time."

"I won't tell them for a while," he said, " But ma'am, it's not safe for your children."

The conversation from this morning flits in and out of my head, a memory stuck there like a song. The kids are playing outside right now. It's safer for them outside.

Monte likes to sit in the brown leather recliner in the living room. He likes to watch football for hours. I hate football. But I love Monte. We've been very happy in this house. I had hoped we'd live here fifty years together, just like Chuck and Irene. Oh Chuck and Irene, how could you be so stupid?

I can still taste the peanut butter residue on my tongue.

I walk through each room like I'm saying goodbye with each closing door. There's the baby blue bathroom with the porcelain claw foot tub. Maybe we could take that with us. We had some good times in that bathtub, me and Monte, when we first moved in.

The children's rooms explode with innocence and stuffed animals and plastic bits and pieces that once were toys. Don't ask me how we are going to pack all that up.

I thought we were happy here. I thought everything was perfect, stable. We were safe and secure. Now I find out it's all on a downward slope. It was an illusion.

I pound down the steps to the basement. I pound down each one with heavy footsteps, like I'm angry at the house because I am angry at the house. I'm angry at Chuck and Irene and their fifty years of bliss.

And where is Monte? Why couldn't he take the day off and listen to the inspector with me? We have a lot to talk about.

I go to the washer and dryer and instinctively change the wet clothes. There's a pile of laundry on the floor and a dead mouse next to it. I swear out loud. I hate this basement. I've always hated this basement. Cobwebs and flooding. Cracks in the floor. When it storms, it pours in through the holes in the walls, like a faucet. Monte and me would go down and try to stop it. The children would run up and down the steps with buckets and throw the rainwater out on the driveway.

I asked Monte to plug up the holes. He tried. He just didn't know what the hell he was doing. Just like Chuck and Irene.

I wander into the storage room and stare at the boxes piled to the ceiling. There's a lot of history in there, a lot of secrets buried under the cardboard mountain, things we've forgotten. What we were like when we were young. What we wanted. What we wore. What we played. The music we listened to. Now we get to open those boxes again, weed through, or throw them away and start all over.

I can hear the children screaming "Daddy, Daddy" at the top of the steps. Monte is home from work. I left the door open. I look up the stairs and see two sets of little arms dangling around his neck as he stoops down. He's standing in the doorway framed by the glow of the fluorescent kitchen light.

Now, Monte may not be the handsomest man. When did he get to be so fat? When did I? But I walk out of that basement and into his arms.

We both start crying. I don't even need to tell him what

happened. He can tell just from the expression on my face. You may ask me, how we didn't notice the foundation was made of wood when we bought the place. We were young and stupid, just like Chuck and Irene.

"It's over," he says. "Isn't it? We have to move on."

Just then there is a rumbling, one of the walls caves in down below and the house starts to sink beneath our feet. The wooden floor starts to crack and drop below us. We just stare at each other, sinking. It feels like an earthquake, the collapse of rotten wood. The children scream and run out the kitchen screen door. It makes a loud slapping sound behind them as it closes. Monte and I stare at each other unmoving, in dumb silence, except for that sound, a strange hissing sound emanating from the basement steps. We are paralyzed by indecision. Should we stay or should we go? Should we run screaming or try to fix it? Can it be fixed? The inspector says it's a lost cause.

"The gas line," I shout over the hissing. "Must have disconnected from the furnace."

Monte stares down the stairs into the darkness.

"Don't go down there Monte. And don't you dare flip that switch."

"I wasn't going to," he said.

My Monte never plays hero, thank God.

We run out of that house as fast as we can. We run into the woods, as far away as we can. I carry one of our children in my arms. He carries the other. And we stand there, our bare feet against the blades of wild grass. We watch from a distance as she ignites, our home. There is a flash and then a slow lingering licking of flames. It is all gone.

But me and Monte, and the children, we're all still here, and as I look over at him, I realize that's the only thing that really matters. The rest can be replaced. Chuck and Irene had their fifty years of bliss, and goddammit, me and Monte, we're gonna have ours.

※

Peter was quiet. Had he fallen asleep? She could feel the rising of his chest next to her. She reached up and touched his face, moved closer to him.

"I'm awake," he said. "I just closed my eyes to see the house, to wander through those rooms. Doesn't feel finished. What happens to them?"

"They live happily ever after," Julie said, with an exasperated sigh. She wanted to throw up her hands but it was too cramped in the car. She was tired. She was hungry. These stories were starting to get on her nerves.

"I doubt that," he said. "Sounds like a metaphor for a shaky marriage, reminds me of Elizabeth. She was never there when it mattered. I wanted to marry her, anyway, you know. I even picked out a ring."

He reached into his pocket and pulled out a fuzzy, little, black box. He opened it and snapped it shut.

"It's funny the little things we carry with us, isn't it?"

What other puzzle pieces were there to this guy? Julie wondered. He still wouldn't give her a straight answer as to why he was out in the storm in the first place.

"You have diamonds in your pockets... You don't happen to have anything to eat in there?" she asked, while opening the glove compartment and rummaging through the cables and bits of paper.

"Nope," he said. "Sorry. All I got is food for thought."

He smiled, and she shot him a look. Her stomach growled.

"Can I see the ring?" she asked. "Don't worry, I won't steal it."

It was an oval, maybe half a carat set on a gold band. He wasn't poor then. In the dark, it was hard to see how clear it was or whether it shimmered. She ran her fingers around the sides, felt the hard diamond in the blackness.

"Try it on," he said.

She laughed. "No, that's okay," she said.

"Please," he said. "I want to know if it fits. I'm curious."

"This might be the closest thing to a proposal I get in my life-time, at the rate I'm going," Julie said, sighing.

"Maybe if we ever get out of here," he said. "Out of this damn car, out of the damn cold, who knows?"

Something about the sentiment reminded her of a Disney movie. What if the two of them were meant to be together? She tried the ring on and it slid right over her knuckle.

"What a strange coincidence," she said. "It fits."

"Must be destiny," he mumbled. "Why don't you just keep it? I don't need it."

"You could return it," she said. She tried to take it off, but the cold metal was stuck around her finger. "Maybe it doesn't fit that well after all."

"I tried to return it," Peter said. "They wouldn't take it back."

"You could sell it," Julie said, still struggling with the ring. She pulled and pulled. She couldn't even twirl it around her finger.

"I don't need money where I'm going," he said.

"What the hell am I going to do with an engagement ring when I'm not engaged?" Julie said.

"Use it to get rid of unwanted men," he said. "Men like me."

"You aren't unwanted," she said, giving him a kind look.

"Just keep it," he said. "Consider it a gift."

"I can't accept this, no way in hell." She looked down at the diamond in the dark and shook her head.

"Yes, you can," he said. "I'm going to die anyway." He gripped his head, where she had bandaged the wound. "I can't take it with me."

"You took a blow to the head," she said. "You aren't thinking clearly."

"So humor me," he said. "Wear my ring. She didn't want to. Would be nice if you were willing for a few hours, before we die."

Julie swallowed. "You know how to guilt a girl, don't you," she murmured. It was getting kind of creepy. She struggled with the ring again. Her head was still resting against his chest. They were uncomfortably close. It was cold and dark inside the car and she couldn't help but shudder against him.

"What if we freeze to death, and they find me in this damn car wearing this engagement ring?" Julie said. "My parents would be so confused."

"So would your boyfriend," Peter said, sarcastically.

"Okay, fine, I don't actually have a boyfriend at the moment," she admitted.

"Aha, so I am unwanted, then," he said. "You thought you could ward off any possible advances from me by lying."

"It just, it just was none of your business," she said.

Things were getting weird again, she thought, putting her glove back on, covering the ring. Her hand was getting cold. The ring would have to stay for now. Ironically, they were bickering like an old married couple in the dark with the lights off.

"From what I hear, marriage is overrated," she said.

"No, it's not," he said. "As long as you love them. Don't you remember what it's like to love?"

"I do remember," she said softly. "It's not something you forget."

"It's impossible to forget," he said. "That's the thing about it that's so maddening. They're all you can think of. I remember when I first met Elizabeth. I'd wake up thinking about her. And the funny thing is you think you have a choice but you really don't. Love is completely outside of your control."

Julie got quiet. He was right, she thought. That is what it's like.

"Do you believe in soul mates?" he asked.

"Not really," she said. "It just seems unlikely that you would have one person out there, just one that was a perfect fit for you and even if there were, what are the chances you would find them? How would you possibly recognize them?"

"I think you'd recognize them. You would know. You would recognize each other somehow."

"Was Elizabeth your soul mate?" Julie asked.

Peter winced in the dark. "If she was my soul mate, she didn't recognize me. No, I don't think so. Hindsight's always 20/20. But she was my first love and there's something special about that.

"Why don't you tell me a story about first love?" he asked. "Innocent love."

"Is love ever truly innocent?" she asked with a smile. "I can tell you a story or two, though. But you might want to hold me closer," she said, pulling the sleeping bag up higher over them. "My teeth are starting to chatter."

He put his arms around her and started to rock slightly back and forth. She could feel the sleeping bag zipper against her cheek and her warm breath mechanically pushing back against the fabric, in and out, out and in.

"It's in first person again," Julie said. "You're gonna take it the wrong way, aren't you?"

"Maybe," Peter said softly. "I'll try not to."

CHAPTER 7
LOVE IN HEELS

used to beat my friend Billy. Well, I didn't actually beat him up. I just pretended. Every day after school, I would jump him on his way to the school bus, climb on his back like I was climbing a mountain. I'd kick him in the butt with my tennis shoe. It was juvenile. It was ridiculous. But it was fun. I'd let out a holler and shriek. Usually, he'd dump me onto the ground. I'd laugh and roll, then wipe off the dirt and blades of grass.

Billy was a varsity football player, so he wasn't easily fazed by violence. He was 6'4 with short black hair and a big stomach. Why I would choose such a large target still astounds me. Maybe because we were old friends since third grade. I could get away with it. I had a fighting nature, a violent side. I was told this was unusual for a girl, but it felt natural to me. When we were younger, I accidentally gave Billy a bloody nose when we were wrestling. I still remember the wounded look in his brown eyes and the way it hurt me down deep in my stomach, almost like I had taken the blow. He had this uncanny ability to forgive me for all my sins.

"It's all good," he'd say and smile.

I missed being the same size. Billy had turned into a boat of a guy, soft and squishy and a mile high. Why wasn't I scared? What was the truth behind all the fake combat? The unprovoked attacks?

Well, obviously I liked Billy. I just didn't know even while he was tossing me to the ground.

I had this realization one night when I was watching Billy on the football field under the sheen of yellow lights. His helmet was in one hand as he walked down the sideline. I was sitting, shivering on the cold, metal bleachers with my friend, Christina, and she turned to me and said in a rather illuminating fashion, "Man, Billy's getting kind of fat."

I hit her against the arm.

"Ouch!" she said, just like a typical girl.

"Don't call Billy fat," I said. "He's just a little squishy."

"You like him, don't you?" she said.

I hit her arm again.

"Ouch!" she yelled louder.

I looked down at Billy standing by the bleachers. He had sweat dripping down the rolls on the back of his neck. I can't remember the score or who they played, but I can tell you the Panthers won because Billy had a big grin spread across his face at the end of the game. He was wearing his letter jacket and sipping water out of a bottle. A black-haired cheerleader gave him a hug. I wish I had dark hair like that instead of red. The hug made me jealous, and I knew he wasn't going to ask me out based on my behavior. I knew I needed to find another outlet, some other way to take out my aggression without physically battering a defenseless football player.

My plan didn't go over well with my mother at the dining table the next day. We were eating bloody hamburgers and glue-like mashed potatoes. "Ma," I said between delectable bites. "I'm gonna take up boxing."

"Like hell, sweetheart," she said. Yes, my mom likes to swear. Where do you think I get the mouth from?

I compromised and decided to take up karate. Once a week I went to a class. I can still feel the wooden floors underneath my feet and the arms of the white robe floating across my forearms as my limbs wound, uncoiled and struck. My leg would travel through the air, slicing and whooshing through it. I didn't mind the bruises blossoming purple and blue across my freckled skin. I'd show them to my friends, wear them proudly like badges. I got a black belt wrapped around my waist. But still, it didn't feel like enough. The violence was too sanitized. I realized I needed more.

I watched the movie Fight Club a million times. There were two problems with creating my own club. A: Men were generally too big for me to fight and B: Girls were pussies. Not to mention the fact that my basement was always flooding and completely and utterly gross.

"Wait," Peter said in the dark. "Her basement floods? Sounds like the last story."

"Be quiet," Julie said. "You're interrupting my train of thought. Just let me tell it."

I flipped through the stacks of college applications and wondered about my future. The way I saw it, if I wanted a real fight, I had two paths I could possibly follow. I could become a criminal or I could become a cop. As much as I liked blood and fighting, I wasn't a bad person underneath it all. Jail wasn't my thing, either. Although I was sure I could find my share of fights there. I'd probably never get out due to bad behavior.

I wished I had a reason to fight. Sometimes, I'd fantasize about a man attacking me in an alley. Maybe he'd make the mistake of tearing my shirt. I'd roundhouse kick him in the face, shoving his nose into his brains. It'd be glorious. He'd drop to the ground and then stagger off, if he was lucky. Like in the old movies, I'd call the cops from a payphone and leave an anonymous tip so he didn't bleed to death in the alley. If I could find a pay phone, that is. The damn things are antiques.

One day at lunch, I found out about a police explorers program in the school newspaper.

"Look, there's a chance to learn more about Tasers and self-defense techniques," I told Christina. "Even ride along in cop cars."

"Awesome," she said, rolling her eyes. "Really, when are you going to give it a rest?"

"Never," I said. I signed up that night and within a week I was in the police station basement, standing in line as a volunteer waiting to be tased with a group of boys. Of course, no other girl in her right mind would show up for such a thing.

I could feel my muscles tightening up, almost spasming while I waited in line with each pop and whirl, as each of the boys in the group was hit. The dart would shoot out from the yellow gun and hit each one square in the back, while two people held him under the arm, as he thrashed, groaned and screamed.

"How do you feel?" the cop leading the program said. His name was Sergeant Steve. "Submissive?"

"Arrrrrggghhhh!" Daniel shouted, a thin layer of drool shooting out of his mouth. The rest of the group laughed nervously.

"It's like riding a roller coaster," Sergeant Steve said. "You think it's going to be worse than it is, but really it's not that bad."

"Not when it's over," Daniel said, plucking the little dart out from his back. "Not bad…"

When my turn came, the boys tried to talk me out of it.

"You don't have to do this," they said. "You're too small, too little. You're just a girl."

"Screw you," I said. "I can handle it."

The shot rang out and I lost control of my arms and legs, sagged to the ground, felt the burning buzz shoot through me, but I refused to make any noise.

"Girls have a higher pain tolerance than boys," I said, shaking my head when it was over. Maybe I lied. It hurt like hell, but I wasn't about to tell them that. I'm sure they could tell from my face anyway. We all wore the same pinched, pained expression on our faces, like our features were squishing together.

"Now, it's time for some self-defense techniques," Sergeant Steve said. Any volunteers?"

I waved my hand in the front of the line.

"Let me show you how to make a fist," he said.

"No, let me show you how to make a fist," I said.

"Let me show you how to take someone out behind the knees."

"No, let me show you how to take someone out behind the knees."

He laughed. "I like your attitude, kid."

I, of course, ended up flat on the mat. But I didn't mind.

"Use what's around you," Sergeant Steve said. "If there's something on the street, a stick, a rock, you grab it."

One day after the class, I got to use some of my moves on a boy named Owen.

"Girls don't belong in the program," he said.

"Fuck you," I said, puffing up my chest.

"You're too little to be a cop, midget."

I was all of 5'2. I threw a punch and busted his lip. The blood blossomed on his face, pouring down his chin. My heart was thumping inside my chest and the adrenaline roared through my arms and legs. He threw me onto the ground. Then he just stood there, touching his lip. "Sadistic bitch," he said.

"Fucking pussy," I called after him, scrambling to my feet.

I cut my red hair into a short bob and got a tattoo across my shoulder blades the minute I turned eighteen. You don't want long hair getting in your eyes during a fight. I'm not telling what the tattoo was, but it sure as hell wasn't a dolphin or a butterfly. Not that I gave a shit, but I'm sure half the school thought I was a dike. But not Billy. Billy knew me well enough to know I liked boys. He had watched my eyes trail after Morgan Taylor's ass on more than one occasion in sixth grade. He used to tease me about it.

It took me all school year, but I got my shit together. I no longer climbed on top of Billy's back and pummeled him with my shoes. But we seemed to have grown further and further apart. By spring, we barely talked. I was busy with the explorers, riding around in cop cars. I wondered if he was busy with the black-haired girl. Skank, I thought, more out of jealousy than anything else. I'm sure she was a wonderful girl.

But I caught him one afternoon in the school parking lot walking to his car.

"Hey Billy, can I get a ride?"

"You aren't going to try to beat me up, are you?" he asked. "You know, I could always just crush you like an ant."

"Fuck you, Billy," I said, laughing. "I'd take you down. You may be bigger but I'm meaner than you are. Besides, I could always kick you in the balls."

"You are mean," he said.

"Sorry," I said. "But don't compare me to an ant."

I frowned, wishing I could curb my tongue and stop threatening him.

"What's the matter?" he asked. "Get in the car."

I sat down next to him on the dirty black leather seat. I had to move a few Mountain Dew bottles to sit down.

"I'm sorry I'm always pummeling you," I said.

"Why?" he asked.

"What do you mean, why?"

"You know, it doesn't hurt much. You're kind of small."

I punched him in the arm as hard as I could.

"Okay, that hurt," he said. "Are you happy?"

"No," I mumbled. I'm fucking miserable, I thought.

"You know, I miss our sixth grade wrestling matches," I said.

"I miss them too," he said, with a raised eyebrow.

"You always lost though," I said.

"I wouldn't now," he said. "But I can still let you win."

"I keep trying to find some healthy ways to channel my aggression without beating the shit out of you," I said.

"I can think of a few ways," he mumbled.

His eyes were downcast but when I didn't say anything, he looked up into my eyes. It was like a lightning bolt struck. He still hadn't started the car.

"You know, I don't really mind," he said softly.

He reached for my hand and slowly uncurled the fingers of my fist.

"I'm going to teach you a few new moves," he said softly. He leaned over and kissed me gently, so gently, I wanted to hit him.

"More," I said. "I want more than that."

"If that's what you want," he said, kissing me harder and pushing himself against me.

"Yes," I said.

Prom came and I got all dressed up in a satiny, purple gown and high heels. The sparkly heels were about four inches tall and chunky. I wobbled on them as I got ready, but I liked the way they put me up high. I hated being short. I liked the way the shoes glittered under the hallway light – pink, purple and gold. They hadn't been cheap.

I checked myself out in the mirror. My hair was short but curled, delicately framing my face. I liked the way my toned arms looked in the mirror. I kept turning and checking out my triceps and the round, satiny sheen of my butt.

I went downstairs and peeked out the living room curtains. I watched Billy step out of the back of a limo. I opened the front door, and we grinned at each other. "You look pretty," he said. I punched him on the arm playfully. I'm not even sure why I did that. Maybe because I wanted him to call me beautiful.

I remember the feeling of him slipping the corsage onto my wrist with his big hands, as my parents took pictures. He looked good in a tuxedo, but who doesn't?

We danced and danced in the school gym. He was such a gentle teddy bear of a guy. I had my face pressed against his chest and we slow danced to every song, even the fast ones. My red lipstick stained his shirt. We didn't say much. It was nice just to be together. We stayed until the very last song.

But it was the ride home that I remember most. I guess I'd gotten used to patrolling in a squad car because I kept looking out the dark window, and I couldn't help but spot a woman fighting off a man trying to take her purse on the sidewalk.

"Stop the car!" I yelled to the limo driver. "Now!"

Billy and I poured out of the doors and the man took off with the red purse clutched under his arm.

"We have to stop him," I said, taking off my glittery shoes and carrying them in my hands.

Billy and I ran and ran. But the man was faster than us, so I stopped and threw my high-heeled shoe straight at his head. The first shoe missed. The second shoe flashed through the air and struck the back of the man's head with a thud. To my amazement, he went down cold.

"Do you think he's going to be okay?" I asked Billy.

"I'm sure."

The woman whose purse was stolen walked up behind us. She had just flipped her cell phone shut after calling the cops.

"Thank you so much," she said, and gave me a little hug.

The cops came within a few minutes. One of them walked up to Billy and shook his hand. "Well, done, kid," he said.

"It wasn't me," Billy said, pointing to me.

"You mean it wasn't the linebacker that stopped him but this little girl right here?" the policeman chuckled. "Even better."

I glared at him. "Don't call me a little girl," I said.

But I couldn't help but smile a bit. Billy and I got back in the limo. I was still barefoot in my nylons with a shoe in each hand.

"So tell me, Amy," he said, putting his hand on my thigh. "When we graduate, are you going to become a cop or a trained assassin?"

"I'm still not sure," I laughed. "But I do know these are my new favorite shoes."

Peter laughed. "It's cute," he said. "So you're a bit of a sadist."

"Am not," Julie said. "It's just a story. My name's not Amy. And I don't like fighting."

"So you changed your name," he said. "Your hair color and your whole philosophy on life."

"Aren't you going to let me have any kind of artistic freedom?" Julie said, gritting her teeth. "It's not about me, dammit. Why do people always think it's about me?" Her leg was bouncing nervously.

"So there's no truth in there whatsoever?" He gave her a funny look. "You don't have a thing for football players?"

"Nope," she said.

"Is it based on any real people?" Peter asked.

"Not consciously," Julie said. "Of course sometimes things do slip through subliminally. Inspiration can strike from the strangest places. But good writing comes from the subconscious mind, at least that's what I think."

"Let me see your palm again," Peter said.

He took off her glove and followed the lines and branches with his pointer finger. His fingers were oddly warm as they danced across her cold hand. "Still can't see it," he said. "But you know, I don't think there's anything in there about becoming a doctor or a lawyer or accountant, definitely not a cop. You're just a writer."

She pulled her hand away from his. She was still wearing his ring. "You know, I think you've got an agenda mister. You just like my stories because you like me."

"Or maybe I just like you because I like your stories," he said.

His lips were turning purple, she realized. Julie looked around the car. It was as though the rest of the world had turned black and white. The interior of the car was black and gray. Even her bright coat seemed to have lost its color. Outside the windows, everything appeared in shades of white, silver and black. Peter was pale in the dark. That can't be good, Julie thought. It was a symptom of hypothermia. They were going to freeze to death, weren't they? Body heat only goes so far. No, she told herself, I'm not going to think about that.

Julie was tapping her foot, arhythmically, trying to regain sensation in her toes. She should have worn those ugly wool socks her dad got her last Christmas, she thought. She reached up and turned on the overhead light. Maybe the engine was dead but the battery wasn't yet. It was strange to be flooded with yellow light, but good, she thought. She stared at the condensation flowing down the windows like tears. Peter winced in the sudden brightness, his eyes narrowing to slits.

"It's not going to make us any warmer," he grumbled.

"We'll be easier to see," she said. "Besides, I like the illusion of warmth."

Outside, everything seemed blacker than ever, but inside was a different story. Her eyes were getting used to the light, and he was coming into focus. He was pale but there was a flush to his cheeks that was kind of beautiful in a way. She noticed an old candy wrapper on the floor, an empty reminder of food they didn't have.

"So we did young love. How about old love," he said. "You have a story about that?"

"Your turn," she said. "I'm sleepy. You tell me one about that. Amy was a hero in love. You got a story about a hero in love? Why do I always have to be the one sharing my stories? I'm sure you've got a few more."

"Well, there is a story about my grandfather," Peter said. "Lord knows what he was thinking."

"Imagine what he was thinking then," Julie said dreamily.

CHAPTER 8
LITTLE THINGS

He stared into the old, oval mirror. He didn't recognize himself anymore. His once blond hair had receded, revealing a pink crown of scalp laced with thin tendrils of white. The skin around his mouth hung in folds and his nose had swollen into a large, red bulb.

Once he'd been a lifeguard doing pushups in front of the beach house at the 57th Street Beach. Now he had a gut. It hung thick and heavy under his T-shirt and blocked the sight of his toes. His chest sagged under the cotton fabric. He ran his hand over the heavy mound of flesh. This wasn't his body. The weight didn't belong there.

Who was this guy? He asked himself.

Had he really changed that much? No. He was the same man. He was still nineteen and rowing his white canoe along the beach with Lake Michigan spread out in front of him like a giant dime shining in the sun. It always seemed to be cold even in August. He could still remember diving into the cold water. He could remember the seagulls cawing overhead, as if he had bait in his boat.

"Arthur?" a woman's voice called. "Are you okay in there?"

It was the only time he got alone these days, in the bathroom.

What was her name, he wondered. Fuck, what was her name? It was the little things that were hard these days. The little things were hard. The hard stuff was easy.

Names had gotten hard. It was like they were there and then withered and wilted in his hands. He found himself wringing his hands trying to remember them, trying to match names with faces like a child's mix and match memory game. The pieces went in and out of focus. He went in and out of focus. The memories flickered and flashed and exploded into nothing.

He came out of the bathroom and there she was. She was familiar, a gray-haired beauty. She took his arm with a gentleness that spoke of love, almost like she was grabbing her own arm, like he was a part of her, belonged to her and always had. He breathed out a relaxed sigh.

"The grandchildren are here," she said, patting his arm.

He nodded and furrowed his eyebrows. Whose grandchildren? He wanted to ask, but didn't.

With small, careful steps, she led him to the pool. He stared at the aqua blue water. He had always loved staring at water, the way it lapped at the edges of the pool, the way the sunlight hit it and sprinkled flashes of white across the surface, and taking in the chemical smell of chlorine. A few leaves had fallen in and slowly floated by. They reminded him of big ships in the distance crossing the ocean.

Two children splashed in the shallow end of the pool, a boy and a young girl. Both blond with pale skin turning a light reddish brown in the sun. They floated by on foam noodles. The girl reminded him of his daughter. His daughter was only three years old though. Wasn't she only three years old? She liked to listen to "pretty music," her words for classical.

A blond woman stood next to him and the gray-haired woman, too. He sat in a patio chair and pulled his hat over his eyes.

"Dad's got to go to an assisted living facility, Ma," the blond woman said, "This is getting to be too much for you."

"We are not sending him to a nursing home," the older woman said, gritting her teeth. "You know what those places are like."

"Assisted living facility," the younger woman corrected. "And they're not all bad. Just think about it."

"Think about it," the gray-haired woman repeated in a terse tone. "Ok, I'll think about it."

Think about it, he thought. Thinking. He wanted to yell at them. He wanted to tell them he was a young man, that he was fine. But the words went in and out, like faulty wiring in his head. He couldn't seem to bring himself to say anything.

"Poor Dad, the dementia has gotten so bad, Mom," the blond woman said. "He can't remember anything anymore. He can't remember us."

He glared at her from under his hat. He had pulled up the brim to look. He felt like a ghost in that chair, considering the way they didn't even turn to look at him.

What does that even mean, anyway? He wondered. Dementia. I remember a lot of things. I was a lifeguard for years. Surely, they were the ones who had it wrong.

The children were oddly quiet, he thought. The boy was toweling off, dripping water all over the sidewalk leading back to the house. He scanned the surface of the pool, but he didn't see the girl.

The two women were still talking, their voices getting louder.

"I'm worried about you, Mom," she said. "I'm worried about Dad, too. He keeps wandering off."

The voices got louder, but he had stopped listening. The water had become too still. Following his lifeguard instincts, he stood up out of the patio chair and walked over to the deep end's edge. He looked down into the water and saw the wavy face of the little blond girl peering up at him from nine feet below the surface with wide eyes. Without a word or taking off his clothes, he dove in and reached for her little torso under the cold water. He pulled her back up to the surface, gripping her slippery torso from behind, underneath the arms. He swam her to the shallow end and carried her up the steps out of the pool.

She was breathing and crying. She wrapped her little arms around his neck. She was shaking from the shock and coughing out water. My little girl, he thought. My little girl.

"It's okay," he mumbled slowly.

The blond woman came up to him and took the child from his arms.

"Oh my God!" she shrieked. "What were you doing in the deep end?"

The gray-haired woman came up to him and grabbed his wet arm, like she was claiming her own child. She kissed him on the cheek. "Well done, dear," she said with a tremble in her voice. He could feel a tear from her face press against his wet cheek. "I'm proud of you."

I still matter damn it, he thought. I still have value. I'm not going to a home. He wanted to scream the words but he was too tired to talk. His mind went in and out. He was out again.

The water was dripping off him and onto the concrete. His clothes felt soggy and cold against his skin. With small, careful steps, she led him back inside and watched as he pulled a pair of dry trousers out from the oak dresser. Where were his socks? Where were his socks? He started opening every drawer. It was the little things that were hard. It was always the little things that were hard. The hard things were easy. The hard things were easy.

She handed him a black pair. He sat on the bed and slowly slipped them onto his feet while she sat next to him and watched. She helped pull on his white polo shirt. She smelled like lavender soap, a familiar scent. She took a towel to his hair, what little of it was left.

They tottered past the old, mahogany table in the dining room, into the living room and she held onto his arm. She grabbed some glossy brochures off the coffee table and threw them into the trashcan by his old desk in the corner.

"Arthur, would you like to dance?" she asked. "It's been a while."

He didn't answer but she hit the buttons on the stereo anyway.

The notes rang out, and he slipped into another state of consciousness full of clarinet and trombone and the rich, gravely voice of Louis Armstrong singing, "What a Wonderful World."

It was the song they used for the first dance at their wedding. What would his wife think of him dancing with this woman? He wondered. He stared down at her gray hair, and smelled the lavender soap again. He tilted his head down towards hers so that his cheek brushed against the soft, silver strands. He closed his eyes and felt the slow steps moving below him, heard the gravelly, rich cream voice, felt the slight shake of her palm against his hand. Her hands were always shaking.

He sighed. Life was good in this moment. He had his good days and his bad days. It was a good day.

"Arthur, honey," the gray-haired woman said softly. "I'm going to dance with you as long as I can."

❄

"I like that he's a hero and we get to peek inside his head as he's slipping away," Julie said. "But it's sad, so sad."

"Do you ever feel like that?" Peter asked. "Like you're slipping away?" Something about his tone made Julie think that it was a feeling he knew too well.

"Not really," Julie said. "I'm too young for that."

"My grandfather slowly slipped away," Peter said, blinking. "He just stopped talking one day. My grandmother loved him anyway, took care of him until the end. He could still dance. There were pieces of him still in there."

"God, that's a sad story," Julie said. Her head was resting on Peter's shoulder.

"Is it?" Peter said. "I'd love to have someone stand by me like that. Love me to the end."

"I wonder what it's like to be old," Julie said. The condensation had built up on the windows to the point where it was rolling down them in streaks. The fog had erased her message drawn on the glass.

"I wonder if we'll ever get to find out," Peter said, his teeth chattering. "I've got a bad feeling we're going to die." He rubbed her arm, like he was trying to warm his own body.

"Eventually," she said. "Not today."

"How do you know?" he asked.

"You've got to have some faith," she said. "That it's all going to turn out okay." She looked up at his face, the white spots on his cheeks, and she wondered if she believed her own words.

"What if you don't believe in God?" he asked.

If there was a God, Julie thought, he was surely an angry one, considering the way the wind was howling outside the car windows. The light inside the car seemed to make the blackness outside all the more complete. White wisps of snow came down in streaks outside the windows.

"I don't know what I believe, to be honest," she said. "But there has to be a reason so many people across cultures and oceans believe. Even if we do die, if we go to heaven, is it really that bad?"

"Heaven and hell, it's just a children's story people make up because they're scared of death," he said.

She pulled her legs closer to her body, so the bulk of her was on his lap, close to his core. She was almost in the fetal position and his arms were around her. It was the warmest position she could find, and yet, her feet were still so cold. Her toes were numb and the sensation was starting to fade from her arches, even her heels.

"Look, I have no idea what the truth is, no one does," she said, shivering against him. "But there has to be a reason so many people believe in heaven and hell."

"I'm an atheist," he said. "I believe in science."

"That's just another religion," she said. "What if you could believe in both? Maybe we're all being too literal. What if whether or not you're happy or sad in your final moment is whether or not you go to heaven or hell, what if that final moment is heaven or hell because that final moment lasts for an eternity? Feels like an eternity? So if you have regrets, it's torture, and if you don't, it's bliss."

"I think the last thought people have is 'Oops, I crapped my pants,'" he said, chuckling a bit.

"Well, that would be hell then," she said. "But I'm sure by that point, you've tuned your body out, tuned out the pain, so it would be the last of your worries."

"Maybe," he said. "But I think you just like to make up stories. Heaven and hell are just good stories."

"Maybe," she said. "Or maybe not. No one really knows."

She closed her eyes for a moment, a break from the brightness. The wind seemed to howl louder. She wondered how they could possibly exist in such an empty moment, such an empty time and space, where there was only white, black and a dimming yellow light.

"What if you go in your sleep?" he asked. "I'd like to go in my sleep..."

"Then you go to heaven with a handful of dreams," she said. "That's the best way to go, don't you think?"

"I don't think there is a good way to go, really," Peter said.

"Maybe you're right," Julie sighed. The light was dimming around them, but it was still on. Julie was thankful for that. She hated the dark. She was thinking about hypothermia again. What did they say on the survival shows? When your body temperature falls, your heart, nervous system and other organs don't work properly. She wondered when that would happen, if it would happen. Would her heart just stop beating? She felt sleepy. That was a symptom of hypothermia, too, wasn't it?

"Do you have any stories about old love?" Peter asked. "I told you one. You've got to have one."

"I do actually, about an old married couple. It's kind of sad though."

"I don't care," Peter said, wiping the condensation off the window with his sleeve. It was a futile gesture. There was nothing to see but darkness and snow. "Tell it anyway. It wasn't like mine was super cheerful either. Anything to pass the time."

CHAPTER 9
THE LAST WORD

This is it. This is the last time. This is the last time I will see my wife, my Marilyn. She's lying in a hospital bed, her thin, gray hair strewn across the pillow in waves. Her face is hollow, skeletal and her lips have turned a purplish blue. Her face is white, so white. I miss the flush that used to creep up on her cheeks. The sparkle has left her eyes. They are dull, brown, and listless and I'm talking to her, and I wonder if she can even hear me. I know she can. But what do words really matter when she's slipping away?

"What do you see?" I ask her, squeezing her hand. She's blinking her eyes. I've always wondered about the way out, whether you really head into a bright white light or if that's all bull like so much they say about the afterlife.

"I see our little Toby," she says softly with a groan. "He's young again. He needs me."

She's delirious, I realize. I will not get any answers out of her. The machines are beeping, the incessant beeping that gets in the way of her sleep but that remind us all she's still alive. She moans. I squeeze her hand tighter. Her fingers are cold to the touch. This time, cancer is the killer.

Toby died almost thirty years ago, from asthma. Her breathing now reminds me of his, loud, labored and wheezy. I remember his curly, brown hair—his eyes, her eyes. I remember the day he was born, how small his feet were, tiny fingers, tiny toes. I remember counting them. How Marilyn couldn't stop smiling, beaming, how her whole face just had this beautiful glow. It's hard to imagine how so many years have passed. The seasons—the summers, the falls, the winters, and the springs—were like the hands of a clock, spinning in time.

I remember her red-faced and angry at me for being late. She was always on time, and I never was. I'd take that anger any day over the silence in the room now. It's silent except for the beeping. What will I do without her? Nothing. I will do nothing without her.

"I won't live without you," I told her on the car ride in.

"Oh yes you will," she said.

"You won't be here to have the final say," I said. And strangely enough, she laughed. How could she laugh? She was so weak I had to help her walk to the car, but she could still laugh.

"You know me," she said, leaning her head back and closing her eyes. "I always have the last word. Always." She let out a deep sigh.

She was so calm even then. Weeks before, she had packed a bag for her last trip, complete with a toothbrush, deodorant, wool socks and a photo album. My Marilyn always did like to plan for everything, even death. And she was always on time and prepared.

She closes her eyes now, and I close my eyes. When I awake, she is still, so still that I wonder if she has died. I touch the skin on her hand and it's cool but still faintly warm. It feels fragile, like rice paper spread across her veins.

"Don't leave me," I bow my head, and I choke on a soft sob. I squeeze my eyes tight and tears flow out of the corners. Back when I was a kid, men weren't supposed to cry, but I'm tired of fighting the tears. I couldn't stop them now if I tried. I'm losing my best friend.

I think back to the day I met her in college. I remember the long skirts she used to wear whirling around her lovely, little ankles. I remember her sitting in the dormitory lounge reading a book, with her legs crossed in front of her, covered in a dark, brown skirt that left everything to the imagination.

I remember asking her what she was reading.

"War and Peace," she said, holding up the giant paperback.

"I've always wanted to read that book," I lied. I never did read it. She teased me about that for years. She even lent me her copy that first year we met. I remember holding it against my chest, all 1,440 pages, and thinking of her when I got back to my dorm room. It was too long. Maybe I should read it now. No, I don't want to. I won't be able to talk to her about it.

I get up and stretch my legs. My stomach growls. I haven't eaten in over twelve hours, since breakfast. I keep forgetting to eat. It's time to hit the vending machine again. I know Marilyn would not approve of the numerous Snickers bars I've been eating. But I don't care. It hurts to be away from her for more than a few minutes. It sends my heart racing. What if she isn't there when I get back?

I get to the machine and it eats my last dollar. I hold back a string of curse words. I walk back to the hospital room empty handed with my stomach still grumbling. She's still sleeping. I sigh in relief.

I sit in the chair next to her. The bed is raised up to help her breathe. There are tubes pumping oxygen into her nose. It all seems kind of pointless, the breathing.

I fall asleep again, nod forward, and wake and then drift off again. I dream of her young and beautiful. I dream of her brown hair, her brown eyes, her laugh. I dream of us sitting in front of the fire. We are in our first home, celebrating something, maybe Christmas. She always loved winter best. She said freshly fallen snow reminded her of diamonds glittering in the sun. We used to get into snowball fights outside with Toby. One time she pelted me in the face. I remember spitting the snow out of my mouth, cold and frozen. "I'm sorry," she had said. "I didn't mean to get you in the face." I had tackled her and thrown her into a snow-drift. She had pulled me down and we had kissed until Toby said, "Eww." We were like children then. We aren't children anymore. But we aren't old either. Marilyn, she's only fifty-seven, and I'm only a year older. Maybe if Toby were alive, maybe if he had grown into a young man, we wouldn't be here, I wonder. Can grief cause cancer? I wonder if any studies have been done.

The nurse comes and checks her blood pressure. Pointless again. "Isn't there anything else we can do?" I ask.

She shakes her head and mumbles, "I'm sorry."

Two days pass like this, pass in a blur. I'm not eating and Marilyn isn't waking up anymore. This is the last time, I think every time I hold her hand. This is the last time, I think every time I kiss her forehead. When will we speak again? Will we ever speak again?

We used to have great conversations. We used to read the newspaper together and argue over politics. She leaned to the left. I leaned to the right. I'll miss our conversations. I'll miss the way she'd call me a "stubborn man." Half compliment, half complaint. I'd call her a communist. She'd scowl but her eyes would twinkle because she was in on the joke. "You know you've lost the argu-ment when you resort to calling people names," she'd say. I always lost the arguments. She was more articulate than I was. It wasn't a fair fight. Her vocabulary was astounding, probably from all that reading she did.

And finally it is the last time. And the doctors and the nurses leave us alone and the machines aren't beeping anymore. The warnings have all sounded and been silenced. She never wanted any heroic measures. She just wanted to go peacefully. And that's how she went, peacefully without a word, into the night, and without a word spoken goodbye either.

I drive back home and open the door to the kitchen, flipping on the light in the darkness. Our cat circles my feet, meowing, but I ignore his lonely cries. I walk up the stairs. I go into our bedroom and I stare at the black safe hidden behind the clothes in the closet. It takes me a minute to remember the code. I punch in the numbers with shaking hands. The door swings wide, and I pull the gun out of the safe, hold the heavy metal in my hands. Trying not to think too much, as fast as I can, I put it up to my head, cock it and click. Nothing happens. I pull the trigger again and nothing happens. I pull out the box for the bullets. It's light as a feather. I open it. No bullets. Just a note in her beautiful cursive handwriting.

"I love you, my dear, forever and ever. Don't even think about it. P.S. Don't forget to feed the cat."

I collapse onto the bed sobbing. I'm crying because Marilyn is right as always. I'm crying because I can't be with her. I'm crying because Toby is gone. She is gone and I'm alone. I also feel a shaking, heaving sense of relief. I was so close to death, but I'm still here. I'm still living. I dry my eyes against the comforter. It still smells of her. I will never wash it.

I wonder where she put the bullets. It isn't until the following spring that I find them in the garden, when I dig up a half-dead rose bush. I shovel up little pieces of steel and dirt. As for the note, it is the last love letter she ever wrote, and I keep it in my wallet, pull it out from time to time, along with her faded picture. My Marilyn, I think with a smile, she always had to have to the last word.

The light had gone out now. Unceremoniously, it had dimmed and dimmed into nothingness. The difference now was that their eyes were no longer adjusted to the darkness. The shapes and forms that had felt so familiar earlier were foreign and abstract once more.

"Really, you said it was sad but you didn't mention all the death. Enough talk about death," Peter said. "I don't want to think about dying right now. We should be lightening the mood. Really, you should have told me something lighter."

"You want happy endings and sunshine," Julie said. "I make no guarantees."

"You're having fun with this, aren't you?" he said. "In a sick way, you are having a good time telling me all about death."

He inhaled sharply. Julie noticed the sound, the sound of their breathing, the rustling of the sleeping bag whenever they shifted their weight, the howling of the wind outside.

"I didn't plan on it," she said. "It was just what popped into my head when you said old love. I can't control my characters."

"You can't?" he said.

"Not really," she said. "It's like dreaming. Do you control your dreams?"

"Sometimes," he said.

"Well it's like that. I'm not used to sharing my stories either. But in a weird way it's kind of liberating, to share." She smiled faintly.

"How many do you have? Stories, I mean."

"Hundreds," she said. "I've been writing since I was a little girl. But only a handful are any good."

"Spoken like a true perfectionist," he said.

"I know," she said.

"Why couldn't she just let him die?" Peter said loudly. "The lady in the story, what right did she have to tell him he had to live without her?"

"I thought you wanted a happy ending," Julie said quietly. "It's important to live while you can."

She placed a hand on the window. She wanted to get out. She wondered how far they were to the nearest town. She berated herself for not paying better attention to the details of a drive she had taken so many times. It was a mistake that could cost her life and his.

"Did you know I've always been afraid of the dark?" she shivered. "And now I'm probably going to die in it."

She wondered what her parents would think after their frozen bodies were found intertwined together in the car. Julie wondered what they'd think of the ring stuck on her finger. She wondered if they were worried about her right now. No, she often came home late. They'd think she'd just have gone out for drinks with the girls again and decided to crash at a friend's house. She did that from time to time. She could feel the fear rising up in her stomach. Her heart pounded warily in her chest.

"I used to be afraid of people thinking I was crazy," Peter said. "But I'm not anymore."

She looked at him for a moment and wondered if he was crazy, if she was going to die with a crazy man.

"Maybe we shouldn't talk about our fears," Julie said, looking over at his face in the blackness. "There's enough to be afraid of right now. Got any last wishes?"

"What I wouldn't give for a twelve-pack of beer right now," Peter said.

"Hell, I'd like a bottle of vodka," Julie said.

"I'd just like to feel loved for once," Peter said. "To be loved before I die. No one has ever truly loved me."

"I'm sorry," Julie said. She didn't know what else to say. "You've still got time, you know. You're not dead yet."

She took his hands out of her pockets and gently blew on them with her warm breath. "Let me tell you another story about love," she said. "Maybe that will help."

CHAPTER 10
THE MUSICIAN

took a shot of vodka and set the empty shot glass down on the tray. It was my second and last of the night. It burned on the way down. The room was swarming with bodies clad in flannel and jeans. I watched them tilt slightly, spin ever so slightly. It was time to lay off the hard liquor, I decided. But I still grabbed a bottle of beer out of the cooler. My hands dipped into the watery ice. Maybe I was nervous.

I found myself walking in his direction. We were at a party celebrating his first record deal, and he was playing in the corner, strumming his guitar and singing softly. "I can't help myself," he bellowed in a sweet, deep voice. Dylan played a C major on his guitar and looked deeply into my eyes. I stopped and stood transfixed. It was a trick he'd used countless times before, I was sure. It was the look you give someone you want to take to bed, and it was hypnotic, but it wasn't going to work on me, not tonight, I thought with a chuckle. I know all your tricks, you silly man. You aren't going to get me with that voice. I don't care how good it is.

He had wild, tousled, brown hair, the kind you want to run your fingers through. In fact, I wondered how many girls had run their hands through it exactly. Dozens, probably. He was a player, and I wasn't about to be played. I don't care if you are a rock star one day, I thought. I don't care if you are singing about love. He was leaving town anyway for New York City. The song, the friendship, would have to come to an end.

He set the guitar down on its stand, and people were cheering, hooping, and hollering. He let out a little smile, a shy smile and I noticed the small gap in between his front teeth. The little imperfections, I find them fascinating sometimes. Why didn't he ever get that fixed? Because he didn't need to. He was still beautiful.

He walked toward me through the crowd. A pretty, blond girl shouted his name and gave him a hug on his way over. His eyes never left mine. He just kept walking through the well-wishers as they patted him on the back and told him congratulations.

"Hey," he said, coming to a standstill next to me. "Did you like my song?"

"Of course," I said.

"Then why were you frowning the whole time?"

"Was I?" I said. "It was a great performance." Maybe that's why I was frowning because it was a performance, because he didn't mean those sweet words, and even if he did, it wasn't about me.

We'd been friends for just over six months now, but there was always something strange about our friendship, a hesitation. I never hugged him hello like I did my other friends. I never hugged him goodbye. We needed a certain amount of distance between us. I know your type, I thought. Best not to get too close. And yet, it was a friendship I enjoyed, and I didn't want to mess it up.

He had offered to teach me guitar. That fall, I had seen him playing outside on campus, softly strumming as he sat on the grass outside with the open case sprawled next to him. A handful of bills and coins sat nestled inside it.

"I wish I could play like that," I had said.

"Let me show you," he had said.

His fingers had pressed mine against the strings, sliding them down the guitar's long neck. I remembered the way he had offered to teach me more, if I came to his apartment. He had more than one guitar at home. Something about the conversation had made me blush. "Maybe another time," I had said. I was always afraid to go. I'm not sure why, maybe I had been hurt too badly by my previous love. Something about him set off my internal alarms. He's going to hurt you. He's going to hurt you badly, I thought. It never occurred to me I might hurt him.

"Do you need another drink?" he asked, and I snapped back to the present.

I held up an empty bottle. "I guess so," I said in a shaky voice. Something about him made me nervous. I could feel it in the pit of my stomach, more than butterflies, more like a sledgehammer to the gut, like I could barely breathe.

He took the bottle from my hand and walked across the room, gently pushing past the crowd, to get me another beer out of the cooler. There were people from wall to wall. He sauntered back with a beer in each hand, and when I took the bottle from him, my fingers brushed against his. A strange, little ripple of electricity shot through them.

With one hand, he reached up and ran his fingers through his wild hair. Something about the gesture got under my skin, maybe because I wanted to run my fingers through it. But no, it wasn't a good idea. He was a dangerous man. He'd love me and leave me, just like all the others before him. I had a track record of getting hurt. And musicians, well, how can you trust a musician? There is something manipulative about someone singing a love song.

"It's kind of crowded in here," he said. "Wanna step outside?"

"Sure," I said. "I could use some fresh air." It felt hard to breathe inside. There were too many people. There was too much warmth.

We escaped onto the porch and sat on a swing hanging there. It was deserted outside. We rocked back and forth slowly in a steady rhythm, our shoes brushing against the wooden floorboards. I held onto one of the chains. I felt warm from my beer. Sleepy even. A part of me wanted to rest my head on his shoulder and tell him all my secrets. A part of me didn't because I had told those secrets before.

"You know, I have a confession," he stammered slightly. "That song, it's about you."

"Is it?" I asked. I blinked my eyes nervously. "You're full of shit." I laughed awkwardly.

"I can't help myself," he said simply. His eyes flitted to my lips, just for a split second.

I stood up and the porch swing swung back. He reached for my hand and pulled me back down gently. I landed a bit closer to him. I could feel the warmth of his leg against my leg.

"What are you so afraid of?" he asked.

"You," I said. "I'm afraid of you. You're going to be a big rock star one day. You're leaving this town and you're going to forget my name."

"Hey," he said, taking my hand. "I'm never going to forget you."

"How do you know that?" I said.

"You never forget your first love," he said simply.

"You can't do this to me," I said. "It's not fair. You leave for New York on Monday. You've known about this for months. What's the point of telling this to me now?"

"The point is I love you," he said. "And you love me too."

"Do I?" I said. I felt myself turning beet red. He was right. I did love him, didn't I? I certainly had all the symptoms. Was love some kind of disease? I wondered. Could you catch it so easily?

"Trust me," he said.

"How can I trust you," I said. "You're a musician, for Christ's sake."

"I'm a human being, for Christ's sake," he said, gritting his teeth.

I looked into his beautiful brown eyes and a small part of me realized I was being ridiculous, childishly fearful.

"Please," he pleaded. "You've got to trust me."

"How?" I said.

He kissed me then. Soft lips against my mouth, warm breath, a tingling warmth, rough stubble. I pulled back and looked into his wild, blinking eyes.

"Okay," I said, realizing I couldn't fight this. "Okay. What about New York?"

"Fuck New York," he said.

"You don't mean that," I said. "You can't mean that. I won't let you give that up."

"Well, come with me then," he said.

That was five years ago. We've been together ever since.

"Is there any truth to that story?" Peter said quietly.

"Maybe a little," Julie said. "I did have a thing for a musician once."

"How did it end?" he asked.

"Badly," she said, with a smile. "But it was fun while it lasted."

"Well, that's good, I guess," he said. "So, why the fairy tale ending then? And they lived happily ever after..."

"You said you wanted a happier story, and maybe I wish it had turned out like that," she said softly. "Maybe I should have gone to New York. I wanted to finish school, but maybe I should have followed him to the ends of the earth. I did love him. We tried for a while. Maybe we didn't try hard enough. I've got regrets."

"It's better to love too much than too little," he murmured more to himself than to her. "You shouldn't have been so afraid."

What if we die here, she wondered. She felt a sinking sensation in the pit of her stomach. "There's so much I would have done differently," she said, "if I could do it all over again."

"I've got my share of regrets too," Peter said, leaning his head back against the headrest and then wincing. "The things I'd do differently if I could just get out of this damn car."

"How are you holding up?" Julie asked.

"I can feel the pain in the back of my head, this throbbing," he said. "Can I have some more of that old water? I'm so thirsty, Julie."

They were both shaking. It was so cold in the car. She was still curled up in his lap like a child. Peter could feel her shivering on top of him, as well. He pulled the sleeping bag up higher. He could see his breath faintly in the darkness. Julie handed him the water bottle, took off her gloves to remove the cap and poured it on his lips. It tasted like plastic against his cottony mouth. A chunk of ice floated round in the bottle. He wished it would melt so he could get more of the precious liquid. But there wasn't enough heat in the car to melt anything.

"We're gonna die in here, aren't we?" he asked, touching his head. He could feel the blood soaking through her makeshift bandage. There was only so much cotton could do. Julie noticed the blood too, touched it with her fingers, oddly wet and warm against the numbness.

"No, we're not," she said.

"Yes, we are," he said. "It's just a fact. No cars have come down this road for hours. The snow around the car is getting higher and higher. It shows no sign of letting up. I can barely feel my hands. We have to leave before we die of hypothermia. We have to go get help."

He pushed her to the side. Suddenly, the car felt too claustrophobic, like the sides were moving closer and closer. It was like the air was growing thinner and thinner. The snow had blanketed all the windows. There was nothing but darkness. His joints were aching.

He swung open the door and stood up. His legs were stiff. It felt good to stand. The cold air and snow pelted his face, pelted his eyes. He felt tears forming at the edges of his vision from the cold. Opening his mouth, he tasted wet snow. He was still so thirsty. The snow was almost welcome.

Julie slammed the car door shut after she got out. She was standing next to him, her hair billowing in the wind, streaking across her face, a blur of snow and blond hair. She raised her hands up against her face, trying to shield her eyes.

"Peter, just a few hours ago, you were dead set against leaving the car, remember? Where are you going to get help from?"

"God, I'll get help from God."

"But you said you don't believe in God."

"Maybe I changed my mind," he said.

"You aren't making any sense. You've taken a bad blow to the head. Peter, you know we have to stay with the car. It's our best shot. All there is out there is fields and fields. It's not like there's a gas station down the road or a house. You'll die out there."

"Maybe I don't care," he said. "If I die."

"I care," Julie said. "I care if you die." She was surprised to find she meant those words. She wasn't just saying that to get him back in the car. Julie pulled his arm. She pulled him hard and pushed him back toward the car.

"Don't touch me." He pulled away from her and kept walking away into the whiteout.

"You're not in any shape to walk out there with your head still bleeding," she said, her voice trembling. "And I'd go but there's nowhere to walk to. Besides, look at my shoes. These are not the kind of shoes you walk through snow in. I'd last five minutes out there. You want to actually die of hypothermia, keep going. In the car, we've got a shot."

He looked down at her feet, her work shoes with the heels, already covered in snow. The leather barely covered her socks. Why were women's shoes always so ridiculously impractical? Elizabeth used to complain about hers hurting her feet all the time.

"Peter, please," she said. "We can't do this."

The wind howled in his ears and he kept walking. The snow circled in front of him, blurring everything to white.

"Stop, Peter. What do I have to do to stop you?" she said. She put her arms around him and hugged him close to her, gently pulling him back again.

"Okay," he said. "Okay, we'll die in the car. I'd rather die in that car with you then die wandering through snowdrifts alone."

"We're not going to die, Peter," she said in a shaky voice. "I promise you."

They turned back toward the car but couldn't even see it in the whiteout. Their feet shuffled through the thick snow. Julie cursed under her breath. It was so cold. She blinked the snow out of her eyes. It was a relief when her hands found the door handle in the white-streaked darkness.

He crawled back into the car. Peter clicked on his seatbelt. It was more of a habit than anything. She crawled in after him. He put his arms around her and held her fiercely tight. The two of them were shaking from the chill. They shook out their legs, brushed off the snow and crawled back under the sleeping bag. But the dampness had done its damage. It was worse than before.

"My dad gave me the ugliest pair of wool socks for Christmas," Julie said. "I never wear them. I wish I was wearing them now. Why didn't I wear boots? Why didn't I pay attention to the forecast? I could lose my fucking toes." Her voice quivered.

Peter was oddly quiet. He was wondering what he had to lose.

"Are you ever going to tell me what you were doing out there?" she said. "Walking in the fields? You must have come from somewhere. Did your car break down?"

"I told you. I broke down," Peter said. "I broke down, and I just started walking and walking, day and night into the country, into the wilderness. Elizabeth left me. I had nothing to live for. And the snow, well the snow seemed to mirror my thoughts. It filled me with a strange, I don't know, ecstasy. I felt like wandering far from home. I felt at home wandering."

"Peter, you need help. Promise me you'll get some help when this is all over. I don't think you are just concussed anymore."

"You think I'm crazy," Peter said.

"No, I don't," Julie said. "I don't mean it like that. I just think you need help. I think you need a therapist or something. Promise me, you'll get some help."

"I promise you, Julie," he said. "I promise you I'll get some help. When this is all over, if we live through it, I'll get some help."

Elizabeth had always wanted him to see a therapist. What good was talking going to do, he wondered. The snow continued to creep up the sides of the car, along the edges of the windows. He could hear the whistling of the wind outside the white Mazda. It was so strong the whole frame of the car seemed to shake now and then. Julie pressed herself closer to him for warmth.

He didn't mind making the promise. There was such a slim chance he'd have to keep it. But when it came down to it, he didn't trust therapists with his secrets. He didn't like telling other people his problems. They never seemed to understand. But the strange thing was Julie seemed to understand.

The two of them drifted off into an uneasy sleep. Peter dreamt of things that were warm. He dreamt he was walking down the beach holding her hand. A few hours later he woke up. She felt cold and stiff in his arms.

"Julie," he said. "Julie, wake up." It occurred to him that her coat wasn't as warm as his and that she wasn't wearing boots.

"Peter," she groaned. "I'm not dead yet."

He exhaled deeply.

"God, I'm so hungry," she said. "I wish I had something to eat." There was this gnawing sensation of emptiness churning within her.

"What I wouldn't give for a warm cup of coffee," Peter said.

"Ahh, a coffee shop," Julie said. It was like they were two old friends in a coffee shop, she thought. The tension between them had melted away. She could almost taste the hot coffee, almost smell it, almost feel the steam rising up and brushing her lips with its warm caress. "I've got a story that starts off in a coffee shop. Two people on a first date. These two have a lot in common, so much so it's kind of scary."

She laughed. Peter liked the sound of it. He smiled in the dark.

CHAPTER 11
FATAL FLAW

She was by no means a perfect woman. There was a reason she was still single.

One of her worst flaws started when she was about three years old, the first time she saw her father hit her mother. Every time he hit her, she bit her nails down to the quick. She even bit her cuticles, spitting out the skin and nails. The fighting and the nail biting continued throughout the bulk of her childhood. Her nails were ragged, jagged and flimsy. They got caught on things, tore and bled. She didn't want to be like her mother, begging a bad man to change. When she grew up, she was going to find the perfect man.

She quit biting her nails in seventh grade, coincidentally, when her father disappeared. She decided she was too old for nail biting, and she just stopped. The decision probably had something to do with a growing attraction to boys. But she still had this habit of putting her fingers in her mouth, an oral fixation. It gave the white tips a thin, washed out look, almost clear and the ridges never went away no matter how much buffing she did. She painted them for years to keep them out of her mouth. She used a hundred different colors, but it never worked.

So it had been about seventeen years since she bit them and yet she found herself sucking on the tips waiting, waiting in the coffee shop for "the man of her dreams." She liked his profile online. There was something funny about it. He liked all the same authors, read the right books, listened to the same kind of music. They even shared the same alma mater, although they'd never met at Yale. They emailed back and forth and she asked him about his GPA. It was the same as hers, 3.89, what a coincidence. She had answered all the right questions in all the right ways on the questionnaire and the computer algorithms had paired them. It made her wonder, if you put all the right criteria in a website, can it manufacture the man of your dreams? Like one of those new 3D printers that spew out children's toys and realistic sculptures?

She had gone through her own manufacturing process, had gone through the usual rituals to prepare. She spent the night before their first date reading about how to catch the perfect man. She had hoisted herself into a pushup bra, wiggled into a tight dress, lotioned every inch of her skin, painted her face to perfection and spent half an hour and a half bottle of mousse fighting off a bad hair day with her industrial strength hair dryer and curling iron. She had even issued a little prayer while she was doing her hair.

"Dear God, please let my hair be good today," she had shouted. She was excited and nervous.

One of her friends had called her that morning.

"You never know what a person is really like when you meet them online," her friend had said. "Be careful, Minnie."

"I'm meeting him at a coffee shop. It's perfectly safe," Minnie said.

"Still, you don't know what his intentions are. Be careful."

"He should be careful. He doesn't know what my intentions are, either," Minnie said, laughing.

"I'm glad you're meeting him in public. He could be a serial killer or something."

"Internet dating is perfectly normal these days," Minnie said, with a sigh. "God you're old fashioned, Liz. A lot of people get married this way, you know, not that I'm in a rush to get married."

"You wouldn't mind it," Liz said.

A few hours later, Minnie found herself in the coffee shop about to embark on a typical twenty-first-century date. Daytime TV was blasting in the corner, clapping and cheering as a man walked in the door. Her heart leapt up as she sprang to her feet.

"Mike," she said hopefully.

"Minnie?" he said.

He came up to her and kissed her on the cheek. Her first impression was positive. He met all the criteria she had listed on stellarmatch.com. About six feet, check. Tan, check. Nice smile with good teeth, check. Hypnotic green eyes, check. He actually looked like his profile picture and all the right boxes were still checked, just like the form she had filled out. He was made to order, one highly selective match. You have to love technology, she thought.

"Do you want anything?" he asked, wallet in hand as he stood by the counter to order.

"No, thanks, I already have my mocha," she said, grinning back at him.

Once he got his cappuccino, he sat down across from her and stretched out his legs in front of him, tapping one foot uneasily on the ground.

What's your fatal flaw, she wondered. What could it be? You look too perfect to be single. Hell, so do I. And so she asked him.

"What's your worst habit?"

He smiled at her. "Is this a job interview?" he asked. "Because if it is, then I'm supposed to pretend a strength is a flaw, say something like, I work too hard."

She laughed, but her mouth formed a small pout.

"You haven't answered the question," she said.

"Why do we have to start out with the bad habits, anyway," he said gently. "Let's start off on the right foot, why don't we?"

"Isn't it strange we have so much in common?" she said. "It's almost too good to be true."

"What's your favorite movie?" he asked.

"Oh, I don't know. I like the scary ones," she said.

"Your favorite then?"

"You're gonna think I'm a freak," she said. "Silence of the Lambs."

"Huh," he said, leaning back and stretching his hands out behind his head in a relaxed pose. "I like that one too. Classic. I saw it when I was a kid and it scared the hell out of me, especially that scene where Hannibal Lector chews off the guard's face."

"I found it scary too," she said. "But I'm pretty good at handling scary stuff."

"So you're not the kind of girl who would dig her nails into my arm during a slasher scene, then?" he said, shifting in his seat. "Interesting."

"Maybe we should go see a scary movie sometime and you can find out," she said, crossing her legs. Nylon brushed against nylon.

"How about now?" he asked. "There's a theater down the street."

"We can walk," she said, sipping the last of her mocha and setting down the cup. Ceramic clinked against ceramic a little too loudly. Her hands were shaking out of excited nervousness.

"You look like such an ideal man," she said. "How are you still single?"

"And you look like the ideal woman. How are you still single?" he asked, laughing.

They put their empty cups on the counter, and he held the door as they left the little café. He had his arm in hers as they walked slowly down the street. She was tottering on three-inch heels, unused to wearing them.

"I'm a bit picky," she said. "When I find something about a man I don't like, I tend to dispose of him pretty quickly. That's why I like to ask up front about bad habits."

"Doesn't that scare them off?" he asked.

"The ones worth having tend to stick around," she said, pulling him closer to her. She liked the way he smelled.

"So I gotta ask you again, what's your fatal flaw?" she purred. "You've got to have one."

"Maybe I don't have one," he said. "Maybe I'm a man without fault?"

"Is there such a thing?" she said, laughing.

"I'll tell you mine if you tell me yours," he said.

"I don't know," she said. "Maybe we should have a little fun before we get into all that." She grabbed his hand and swung his arm, practically skipping to the box office.

They sat through the slasher movie, sat through the bullets and the blood and the gore. They sat through the fire and the explosions, and she didn't jump once. She held his arm but didn't flinch. He didn't flinch either.

But as they were walking out of the movie, she caught his glance follow the behind of the girl in front of them. She didn't like it. That's it, right there, she thought, staring at the girl's short shorts. He's a cheating bastard, isn't he? Just like the last one.

"Where to next?" he asked. "Shall I walk you back to your car?"

"Yes," she said, winding the red scarf around her neck.

"How about we take the riverfront trail back?" she said. "I'm not in a huge rush, are you?"

"Not at all," he said, raising his eyebrows.

"Such a charming downtown area," she said. "I love the old fashioned streetlights."

He was encased in a yellow halo of light. Rows of 1920s buildings surrounded them, only a couple stories tall, with arches over every window that made it seem like the old buildings had eyes and eyebrows. They seemed to have their own souls when you looked at them for a while.

"So why do you like slasher movies, so much?" she asked.

"I don't know. I guess I just like cheap thrills."

"I usually like something a little more cerebral," she said.

"I know what you mean," he said.

She was playing with the tassels on her scarf and winding it through her fingers.

"What else do we have in common?" she asked.

"I don't know," he said. "You have any pets?"

"Me and pets don't get along," she said. "I used to chase my parents' cat around the house with a fork."

"That reminds me of the children's story, Where the Wild Things Are," he said. "The little boy chases the dog around with a fork. I used to love that story."

"Me too," she said. "That's where I got the idea. God, that's eerie you picked up on that."

They were both children of the '80s, that was for sure, she thought.

"I'm pretty familiar with the story. My mom used to call me a wild thing, and lock me in my room for hours," he said. "All I had to do was read books by myself."

"That sounds sad," she said. "I'm sorry."

"She wasn't a very nice woman," he said. "I'm still angry. I don't know why I'm telling you all this, anyway."

They had walked down the steps and were on the trail now. The sun was long gone and the river was a dark gray silver, twinkling under the lamplights. She liked the way the light reflected on the churning river snaking next to them. There was something elegant about it, so close and so deadly. The water had claimed three lives within the last year. It made her shudder to think of it. Boulders lined the path, and she pulled him closer to the concrete edge, the rail.

"So you still want to know my secret?" she said. "Why I'm still single?"

"Your fatal flaw, as you call it?" he said. "I'll tell you mine if you tell me yours?"

He reached for the end of her scarf, and she gave it a little tug to release it from his grasp. "Oh, so you like scarves, do you?" she asked.

He wound the scarf around her neck and unwound it in a toying gesture. She gripped at it and pulled it away from his fingers.

"Not so fast, mister," she said. "It's my turn."

She ran the scarf around his neck. "You ever heard of auto-erotic asphyxiation?" she asked. The comment usually bought her some time.

"That's very dangerous," he said.

"Do you like that kind of thing?" she said, pulling the scarf tighter around his neck and standing behind him.

"I'm not into strangling," he said hoarsely, pulling the fabric from his neck.

That was when he pulled his knife out of his pocket, flipped it open and thrust it out behind him, at her.

Minnie leapt back and laughed and laughed when she saw it. It was a funny thing to bring on a first date. His face flushed red like she had somehow emasculated him.

"What's so funny?" he asked.

"Nothing," she said. "I'm very scared."

"Then why are you fucking giggling? I could kill you."

It was then that she pulled the handgun out of her pocket.

"Not if I kill you first."

"I've never had this happen before, on a date," he said.

"Neither have I," she said. "I keep thinking that the computer algorithms have gotten awfully advanced. Everyone always jokes about an online date with a serial killer…"

Her gun was still pointed at him. "Can you guess why I'm still single?" she said.

"You like to kill men," he said.

"And you, you like to kill women, don't you?"

He coughed and nodded.

"Tell me, when two serial killers go on a date, is it a perfect match or does it end with bullets and bloodshed?"

"I don't know," he said. "Maybe if you put down your gun and I put down my knife we could give it a try."

He threw his knife into the river with a gulp and eyed her gun.

"Forgive me if I hold onto this for a while," she said, slipping it into her right pocket. "You are a bit bigger than me."

"How are we supposed to trust each other?" he asked.

"I don't know, maybe that's part of the thrill," she said, taking his hand. The two of them walked along the riverbank.

"They should really rename that website," he said. "Stellar-match.com doesn't cut it."

"It should be killermatch.com," she said, laughing. Who knows, she thought, maybe he was marriage material, after all.

"Tell me about your first time," she said.

"Her name was Melissa Jones," he said dreamily.

"Not that type of first time," she said. "Your first kill." She was excited to meet someone she had so much in common with.

"It was one and the same," he said. "Melissa's parents died in a car accident a few years before I met her, and she wanted to be with them but she was too scared of death to do it alone," he said. "She was my first love and one night I told her, I'd do anything for her. 'Anything?' she said. 'Anything' I said, and she told me that I could make love to her if I promised to slit her wrists afterward. So I did. I spent my first time thinking about how this was the last time I was going to kiss her lips, her breasts, press my thighs against hers...."

"Too much detail," Minnie said.

"Anyway, I didn't know how I was going to do it, but she made it so easy. She took some pills and held out the knife in one hand. I took the knife, kept it pressed in her fingers and cut along the vein. I watched as the blood left her body and her face faded into a soft violet shade of pale I had never seen before. I didn't cry because she was smiling. She was happy to be with them again."

"That's almost sweet," Minnie said.

"I do it out of love, you know," he said. "I'm a collector of hearts, beating and broken. I like to put women out of their misery. That's my type. The way I look at it, it's an act of kindness really. I'll be whatever you want for a night, be your dream man, and then I end it without any tears. Love heals all wounds, and I love for one night."

"That's sick and twisted," she said. "But I can relate."

"A lot of people love for one night but with a lot less finality," he said. "Why leave the woman the next day? Think about it, she never has to wake up alone again. No more rejection. She gets to live forever, entombed in my glorious basement, her heart in a jar."

"I don't want your type of kindness," she said, gritting her teeth slightly. "So you didn't go to Yale. That makes you a liar. I like to kill flawed men, especially cheaters. That's my pathology. Are you a cheater?"

"Nope," he said. "Never been in a relationship long enough to cheat. How do you end up with so many cheating men?"

"I attract the wrong type, I guess," she said with a sigh. "I'm tired of killing men. I wish I could find one worthy of keeping alive."

"Maybe you like the wrong type. If you're tired, maybe I've got a solution for you," he said.

"That would be…"

"Death, of course," he said, laughing.

"I'm not feeling particularly suicidal but thank you, Dr. Kevorkian." She laughed and squeezed his hand. "I'd rather just find the perfect man."

They were back in the parking lot, and she unlocked her car.

"Are you going to give me the axe, or let me come home with you and stay the night?" he asked.

She couldn't help but giggle as she leaned against the car door. "Maybe both."

She whispered her address into his ear and kissed him, biting his lower lip. For a moment, she wondered if she had finally found the perfect man. If not, well, there was a hatchet under her pillow. It would be there waiting for him with a red ribbon tied around its wooden handle.

"Oh come on, you've got to be effing kidding me, not even a little blood and guts? And you avoid the sex scene…" Peter said, his breath rising cold in the dark. "Why?"

"I don't know," Julie said, blinking her eyes, trying to get used to the blackness inside the car again, after the burst of white snow.

"Have you ever tried your hand at writing about forbidden love and sex? Romeo and Juliet? I bet you'd make a great romance novelist, if you gave it a try."

"I'm no good at those stories," she said, her teeth chattering. "Not enough experience really."

"Make it all up then," he said. "Don't hold back. Why are you holding back?"

He still wasn't wearing his gloves. He put his hands in Julie's jacket pockets.

"Aren't your fingers cold?" she asked. It was all shadows and darkness in the car.

"They're warmer in your pockets, closer to the body heat," he said. "Which reminds me, you know I'm sure the survival shows say we should take our clothes off and snuggle to stay warm."

Her head was on his shoulder, and she lifted it to face him.

"Oh for the love of God! How can you even think of getting naked at a time like this when it's so damn cold?" She squirmed on his lap. "I can't even feel my feet or my hands anymore. The last thing I'm going to do is take off clothes."

"Skin against skin is always the warmest," he said. "You can trust me. I'm not going to try anything. You know that. Come on. Do you usually distrust all men?"

"Men are generally untrustworthy in my experience," she said.

"Let's not be silly. We are two adults, here. Why not have a little fun in our last moments?"

"How hard did you hit your head again?" she sighed. "How can you possibly be thinking about sex at a time like this?"

"If you're going to go out, why not go out with a bang?" he said, laughing. "No, I'm just kidding... Unless you're interested of course."

"No way in hell," Julie said. "Sexy story maybe, but actual sex, hell no."

She was cold, but he was shaking. She could feel his muscles shuddering against her, fluttering against her. They still felt warm but how much longer would that last? She could feel the warmth of his breath against her cheek. She wished she could pull away from him, but it was impossible. They both needed the warmth. She knew it was going to hurt when they warmed up again, that her feet and hands would burn when the sensation returned. It would be a relief, but a painful one.

"Anything to get my mind off dying in the cold," he said. "And don't be afraid to throw some sex in there."

"Fine, you want Romeo and Juliet," Julie said, gritting her teeth slightly. "I'll give you Romeo and Juliet."

CHAPTER 12
THROWING STONES

The first day she had seen him, she had asked him his name, and it had told her everything she needed to know. He was from a Muslim family. Her Hindu family would never accept him. Her family would never have faith in his faith.

She knew she shouldn't want him. It was dangerous and wrong to play with a man she wouldn't be allowed to marry. And yet she did want him, even if it was against the rules. She wanted to feel his hands running up and down her body, his breath on her bare shoulders, hot on her neck. She wanted to tangle his long, wavy black hair around her fingers.

He had dark brown, hypnotic eyes. His skin was tones of olive and gold and... his smell. She could lean in and smell him and feel alive.

They met on the beach. She found him along the shore one day skipping stones. She wanted to ask him to show her how, but she couldn't. She watched his flicked black stone skim the blue surface and hop joyfully across the water. When she tried on her own, the stone sank. She picked up a cold, wet piece of glass that had been frosted and rounded by the waves and wondered what that would feel like, to become such a stone.

She felt like she was all rough edges. She felt weak and sharp. The words never came out. At first, she just sat there with him in silence on the bench by the old, rotting wooden pier. Never sure what to say, what not to say. But her eyes betrayed her. His eyes did too. The way he looked at her, like it hurt him to look, and yet he had to look. The way he winced at her beauty. It spoke a thousand words.

It was safe in the silence. She could imagine it was nothing, just her imagination, just two people skipping stones at dawn. She wondered if he'd come back just to see her every day? If he was always there at the same time or if he just loved the water, not her at all? They kept watching the sun rise together. They kept watching it break across the water, spilling gold across the waves.

"Can I show you how to skip properly?" he asked on the third day, breaking the silence that had come after she had asked him his name. "You need the right kind of stone, a flat one. You have to arc your wrist like this." He held her hand and she felt her knees go weak as he wound her wrist back and forth and swayed her arm. After a moment, she pulled away like he had hit her.

"Do you live around here?" he asked.

She nodded.

"Want me to walk you home?" he asked.

"You know I can't be seen with a man like you," she said, looking up and down the beach. "It's better if you leave me alone."

He winced but walked away. He knew the rules, too.

That night she was unable to sleep. She just kept rolling and turning in her bed, wrapped up in blue sheets. The whoosh of a ceiling fan reminded her of the waves. The clouds were rolling in. The wind was building outside. When it came down to it, she knew almost nothing about him, just that he liked to throw stones. And she wanted to hate him. She wanted more than anything to hate him, to forget him. This is my life, she thought, a mess, a tangle of sheets.

She unwound the sheets and got out of bed. When she got to the pier, he was already there, skipping stones across the waves before dawn. The rocks jumped across the dark, silvery water.

He tried not to look her in the eye as she walked by. His eyes stung as they stared and blinked down at the sand, but the moment she passed, he looked up and watched her walk away. She had small, white flowers in her black hair.

He started walking behind her, reached for her arm. She turned and shook his hand off her. "I can't," she said. "I don't want to talk to you. I can't talk to you."

"Why not?" he said.

"Not a good idea," she said.

"What's the worst that could happen?"

The wind whipped his black hair over one of his eyes and she wanted to wipe it away, wipe it back. Would it kill her to reach up and touch his hair? Would it kill her to touch him? She wondered.

"I don't know," she said.

"What are you afraid of?" he asked.

"I don't know you," she muttered. Why couldn't she just keep her eyes off him, she wondered. She stared at the sand. She looked down at the dark silvery water lapping her sandaled feet, down at the rocks, the tangled green black seaweed, crab claws, the stones, trying not to look at him in the dim morning light.

"What do I have to do to get your attention?" he asked. "To stand a chance."

She didn't answer.

"Marry me," he said breathlessly.

She laughed. "You're joking," she said.

"You could marry me. I'd do anything for you."

"Would you?" she said. "Do you know what I'd have to do for you, for a stranger, if I married you?"

He looked down at the white sand and seashells.

"I'd have to give up my parents, my aunts and uncles, my cousins, my grandparents. I'd have to forget everyone else I ever loved to be with you. I'd have to kill their love to get yours. They'd never approve."

"My family would accept you. But if they didn't, I'd walk away from them as long as I had you."

"And my faith, would you accept that?"

"And your faith."

"You don't know me. You're playing with me. I can't give up my family," she said. "It's not that easy. I don't even know you."

"I feel like I know you," he said. "I'm not playing. Let's just talk for a while. Walk with me."

They walked for miles along the beach. The sun was just starting to split silver and gold across the sea. The fishermen were casting their nets out on the water. They were distant figures, outlines, in their boats.

"I'm studying to be a doctor," he said. "I'm a respectable man, you know."

"Are you?" she said, laughing. "I haven't decided what I want."

"What kind of man you want or what you want to be?" he asked.

"Neither," she said. "I'm still young."

"How young?" he asked.

"Nineteen."

"Ahh, a rebellious teenager. I'm twenty five."

She said nothing, just crossed her arms.

"You ask me a question, now, anything at all," he said.

"What are you most afraid of?" she asked.

"Watching you marry another man," he said.

"You're a man with an agenda," she muttered. "I don't trust you."

"So you're most afraid of me, then?" he said playfully.

"No, I'm most afraid of wild dogs," she said, smiling. "Are you a wild dog?"

"Maybe," he said.

The air smelled of salt and they came across the old chapel. It was one of those relics from the Portuguese, small, wooden and weather-beaten with a gray cross hanging on top, slanted with gold paint flaking off. He pried a board off the side of the window and hopped inside.

"Want to see?" he asked. He pulled her by the hand over the window ledge.

Why did she feel so at ease with those dark eyes and that warm voice?

"Have you been here before?" she asked.

"Yes," he said. "But I've never brought a girl here, if that's what you're wondering." He chuckled.

He flipped the light switch and a few light fixtures lit up the room: burnt-out bulbs and chandeliers dotted the hallway. She was surprised by the flickering electricity.

"You could marry me here," he said.

"But we aren't Christian," she said.

"A technicality that works in our favor. We don't have to choose one faith over the other, a new faith," he said. "Marry me."

"How?" she said. "There isn't a priest here."

"There's no one here," he said.

"Marry me now," he said, pressing his body against hers in the hallway, tugging at the white flowers in her hair until they fell onto the floor.

"I can't," she said, touching his hair. God, it was so soft in her fingers.

"Please," he said. "Any vow you want me to take. I'll take it."

It was quick. It was so quick that first kiss darting across her throat, flashing across her lips. She could feel his chest pressed against her breasts, feel her back pressed against the wood paneling in the dimly lit hallway. His face was cast in a yellow glow, glowing against the rich red of the mahogany wood paneling behind him, behind her. It was the smell of dust and floorboards and nervous sweat and old lights. It was the smell of skin closing in on skin. He looked golden against the old lights. His lips, his nose, the way the light caught in his black hair.

He unbuttoned her top, trying to unpeel her layers. At first she shook her head to one side but no words came out, and she didn't stop his hands or hers from their wandering. It felt like he was searching for a way under her skin, like he wanted to live within her and wanted her to live within him. And that didn't bother her as much as it should have because it was only for a moment. That's what she thought. No one can live within you forever. That's what she thought.

It was a strange thing the way zippers and buttons fell away and fabric unfolded and unfurled so naturally until it was just the two of them in that hallway. Soft, bare skin pressed against wood paneling. He held her hand above her head, clasped her fingers within his in a strange kind of prayer and pounded her against the wall until the dust shook off the light fixtures, and floated down silver, almost like a gray mist falling on them. Ashes to ashes, she thought, dust to dust, a funeral of sorts because the moment, the "marriage," wouldn't last, even though they wanted it to.

And he was so beautiful with those angel arms holding her hands above her. And the way he looked into her eyes, like she was the only woman in the world. She threw her head back and tried not to scream, tried not to cry, and he buried it all in a kiss. He buried it all in a cascade of kisses. Ashes to ashes. Dust to dust. Kiss after kiss. Stone after stone.

He was sinking, and she was skipping across the water.

He was sinking, and she was a skipping stone.

Julie blushed in the dark. It felt like she had shared something intimate with him. It was as though they were two dreamers sharing the same blanket. Peter said nothing for a moment. "But they barely know each other. How could they possibly love each other?" he said softly.

"It seems to be a theme, doesn't it," she said.

"Impossible love," he muttered.

Was he talking about the characters or the two of them, she wondered. The lines were starting to blur in the darkness, with the fatigue. She took off a glove and stroked his cheek with the back of her finger. It was a strange little gesture. Affectionate but not sensual. It felt like they had already done that part. "Love at first sight," she muttered. "Has that ever happened to you?"

"Maybe. Like I always say, hindsight's 20/20," he said. "It's not always possible to tell in the middle of something like that."

She rested her head on his shoulder. "Tell me more about yourself, Peter," she said. "I'd like to know more about you. I feel like you know way too much about me, through my stories."

"I really don't know that much about you, and there isn't enough time," he said, staring at the clock in the car. The display was blank, lifeless without the car battery. Peter looked down at his watch and grimaced as he moved his head.

"Why don't you tell me more about Elizabeth," she said.

"There's not much to tell," he said.

"How did you meet her?" Julie asked.

He paused, thinking.

"Sometimes, I wonder who was to blame," Peter said softly. "Was it my fault or her fault that I loved her? What was it about her that made me love her so much? Sometimes, I try to find the exact moment it started.

"We were just kids back then, in college. I saw her in the Helen C. White library immersed in a book, her long black hair falling forward as she read, To Kill a Mockingbird. She looks up at me with these sparkling green eyes, and I feel the rest of the world disappear.

"She smiled at me and kept reading. She hadn't even spoken. It only lasted a second. I didn't know what to say to her, if I could say anything. I knew I had to say something. I set my bag down and pulled up a wooden chair to the table. There she was diagonal from me and suddenly I saw it, a tiny, black spider dangling in front of her face. Her hand had been pressed against her forehead while she read, hunched over, and the spider dangled below her fingers. There it was helplessly swaying inches from her skin.

"'You've got a spider dangling from your hair,' I said. She looked up and saw it. She stared at it for a moment. It was actually attached to her hand by a silver string. She watched it, totally fascinated, not afraid, and then it dropped and ran across her arm. I watched it disappear, and I knew I looked a little too long, eyeing her arm a little longer than I should have, admiring a small part of her while I could.

"She did it then. She looked up at me. She had a way of locking eyes with me, a way that made me feel like I was the only person in the room. Maybe that was my imagination. But I felt like the spider then, small and helpless. I felt like running away. She had so much power over me, even then. She was the puppeteer and I was the puppet. I was attached by a string.

"'What's your name?' she asked.

"'Peter,' I said.

"'Like the children's story,' she said softly. 'Peter Rabbit. I don't know what makes me think of that.' And then she laughed like music. I loved the sound of it, and that was how it started."

"And how did it end?" Julie asked softly.

"The usual way. We got into a fight," Peter said.

"Like a fist fight?" Julie asked.

"No, like an argument. Why would you think a fistfight? You think I'm a violent person?" He inhaled sharply.

"No," she said. "I didn't mean it like that."

"I never got a chance to propose you know. She found the ring on her own, rifling through my sock drawer. She was always stealing my socks. Never had a girlfriend who didn't."

"You should have found a better hiding place," Julie said.

"Why hide your heart?" he said. "I was still trying to think of a way to ask her. But all I could think of were clichés. I had gone through a list of things I could do, a scavenger hunt, a romantic dinner, a live band. I even toyed with doing it at a baseball game, asking her to marry me on one of those big screens. Elizabeth loves baseball.

"I came home and she was waiting for me at the kitchen table with the ring in its little black box in her hands. She kept opening and closing it. I could feel a twinge in my heart every time she snapped it shut. There was something so final about that noise.

"'I'm not ready,' she said. 'I want to be free.'

"I didn't take it well," he said.

"I'm not surprised to hear that," Julie said. She stared at the condensation on the window. She was tired of wiping it off. There was nothing new to see outside anyway.

"Then what did she do?" Julie asked.

"She left. She said she had met someone else. She said she was tired of me being down all the time. I just couldn't take it so I started walking. I wanted to get the hell out of the apartment we shared.

"I walked out in the dead of winter, just started walking and walking," Peter said. "There was something about the snow that seemed to mimic the way I felt. It was cold, frozen and whirling and I just went walking in it. I didn't care about freezing to death. I didn't care about anything. I just wanted to walk, to get away from it all. I just went numb after a while. It crept into my fingers and toes and then it seemed to spread from there."

"Did you want to die?" Julie asked. "Is that why you jumped in front of my car?"

Peter didn't answer. He didn't even shake his head. "I had a breakdown," he said. "That's the easiest way to put it. I wasn't thinking clearly. I wasn't thinking about anything or anyone. I felt like everyone would be better off without me. All I could think about was the hurting, the aching in my heart, and I wanted it to stop somehow, and I felt like if I just kept moving, if I just kept walking I would get to the end of it somehow, that I would find a way to end it."

"Damn, Peter. That's not good. Promise me you'll get some help and live your life after this," Julie said, adjusting her position to look him in the eyes. She put a hand on his shoulder. "You need help, like professional help. There's no shame in that. You have to survive. Promise me."

"Only if you promise to finish your book," he said, with a sad smile. "Why don't you promise me that?"

"Okay," Julie said. "I will. Just don't expect it to be any good... God, I'm tired."

"Don't go to sleep," he said. "Stay awake and talk to me for a while longer."

"I think it's been long enough," she said. "You can go to sleep again. You need your rest. The bleeding has stopped. We just have to wait for help to come, for the day to break. We have to wait for the storm to calm down."

"Don't sleep," he said. "I don't want you to sleep. I'm afraid."

"I'm afraid too, but what's the point in worrying about it?" she asked.

"Thank you," he said. "You've been a friend to me in a dark time."

"Don't thank me," she said. "I've done nothing but try to make up for the fact that I hit you with my car."

He laughed at the ridiculousness of the statement and she liked the sound.

She snuggled closer to him, for the warmth. It was a strange feeling to be so close to a stranger. But she felt like she knew him now. They had traded so many stories.

"I can't die until I write my book," she muttered. "I can't. I still haven't finished it. Maybe a little unfinished business is a good thing."

"There's nothing more tragic than an unfinished story," Peter said.

She thought about getting out, but she was too tired to unbury the car, too cold, so she let the snow cover the glass. She curled up against the hitchhiker's chest and went to sleep. She dreamt of angels.

He was checking his watch when the hands landed on four a.m. She had left the key in the ignition and the other keys on the chain swayed slightly. So I was wrong, he thought, with a smile. Maybe I'm not a psychic.

She was curled up against his chest like a child. He had been playing with her blond hair, winding it around his fingers. Maybe that was creepy of him, but he couldn't help it. He'd caress it and then put his hand back in her pocket. She was beautiful. He loved the soft sound of her voice, the way she told her little tales. Something about their conversations made him feel lighter, more at peace. Or maybe it was the possibility of death coming soon.

His watch could always be fast, couldn't it? The windows were covered in snow. The drift had blown over the car and buried even more of it. Wisps of snow travelled on the wind, like sand blowing over a dune.

Then he heard the scraping noise behind them, the grumble of an engine.

She was sleeping when the plow came, not that it would have changed anything if she had been awake. He saw the flash of white light against the glass. He had seen it rise up and over their shoulders, casting their figures black like shadow puppets. There hadn't been any time to react. But she had made a sound, a whimper, a cringe and then the impact of metal against metal, jarring, tossing his head around like a toy, a doll with its head about to snap. Except his didn't snap. And there was glass all around them, flying like diamonds, flying like the snow outside. And she was flying away like an angel, her arms out like a bird's wings trying to catch her fall as she crashed through the glass and soared out of the car. Something about it all fluttering around him reminded him of Christmas, reminded him of ornaments on a tree, red and white, and sparkling and shining. The metal twisted around metal.

Pieces of paper flew from the back seat, sheets of it, old receipts like doves fluttering through the air. Or did he imagine that?

CHAPTER 13
THE LAST STOP

He woke up in the hospital with tubes in his arms. His shaky finger reached up to brush back his hair from his face and instead touched the gauze wrapped around his head. His throat was sore. He wondered how much time had passed since they had taken out the breathing tube.

He recalled screaming silently, a scream that breaks at your lips and stays there and dies with a breath. Help! Even now, in the hospital, he wanted to scream but he couldn't do it, because the timing was off. Such things are better done in the moment. His fingers fumbled on the side of the bed, looking for the buttons. He raised the bed up. He lowered it down.

Goddammit, he thought.

It hurt to crane his head. Something was pulling at the base of his skull, the bottom of his neck. He wanted to touch it, but he was afraid. He struggled to look at the rail on the bed and hit the right button. There it is. It says, Help. Thank God. The nurse will come. Help will come.

He pushed it once, twice, three times, and nothing happened.

"The button doesn't work," a voice said next to him. "It's been disconnected. You're in the psych ward. The help button doesn't work in the psych ward."

"What happened to her?" he asked in a creaky voice.

"Who?" the man's voice said. He was on the other side of a closed, white curtain.

"The woman in the car with me," Peter said.

"I don't know," the man said. He wheeled into view. He was dark haired and pale, sitting stiffly in his wheelchair, just outside the white curtain partition. "You want me to call the nurse?"

"Yes," Peter said in a tired, raspy voice. He had almost nodded but had stopped just in time. His head still hurt.

"Delores!" the man shouted in a deep voice.

"Yes, Max?" a woman's voice called from the hallway.

"Delores! Peter wants to talk with you again."

She walked in with her clipboard, her pen on a string around her neck, in a pair of scrubs that hung loose off her body, as baggy as a prison jumpsuit—but in a respectable violet print rather than orange.

"What happened to Julie?" he asked, his voice breaking with the words.

"Peter," she said, softly, sitting down in the chair next to his bed. "We've already had this conversation ten times this week. You wrote it down, remember?"

"What happened to the woman in the car?" he growled.

"Look, I don't want you to keep fixating on her," Delores said, patting his arm. She was not afraid of him, he noticed. Maybe he was too weak to be a threat to anyone anymore.

"Don't baby me," he said. "I hate it when people baby me. Where is she? Is she here? Down the hall? I'd like to see her."

"No, Peter, she didn't make it. You know that."

"She told me stories, you know," he said, wincing, trying not to cry. "She told me these wonderful stories to keep me awake that night."

"Did she?" the nurse said, sighing.

"They were from a book," he said. "I'd like to get a copy. The Book of Impossibility."

"I know, Peter," the nurse said. "I already brought you a copy. It's from the library so don't wreck it. It's a magic book."

"How will I remember to return it?" Peter said, looking up at her from his bed.

"I'll remind you," Delores said. "You'll be here for a lot longer than the two-week borrowing period with the kind of problems you've got. You keep forgetting to eat for Pete's sake. You keep repeating the same stories. We can't have you leaving like this."

She put his notebook and pen on the little desk attached to the bed and pushed it toward him. Then she sighed again and turned to walk out the door.

"Thanks, Delores," he said. He was always polite to nurses. Maybe because they reminded him of his mother, the way she used to take care of him when he was sick.

He picked up the red notebook and opened it to the first page.

"Now, I remember," he said out loud. It was a lie, but it was the truth.

It was evening, what seemed like days later, when the psychiatrist came to visit. He was a short man with dark lines of hair on his arms and little, round glasses, and some kind of accent. Peter stared at the man with suspicion. His memory was coming back. What would the interrogation be about this time? It was always the same, and it always got him riled up right before he was supposed to go to sleep.

"What were you doing that night, out walking around in the cold in the middle of a storm?"

"Nothing," Peter would say. "I was doing nothing."

"Tell me about your job. What happened at the bank?" the doctor would ask.

"Nothing," Peter would say. "Nothing happened."

"What happened with Elizabeth?" The doctor would ask.

"Nothing," Peter would say. "Absolutely nothing."

"What are your plans for the future?" The doctor would ask.

"Nothing, absolutely nothing," Peter would say.

It was the wrong answer. The man scribbled something on his pad. "Have you ever had any thoughts of suicide?"

"Of course," Peter said. "Hasn't everyone?"

But tonight, the psychiatrist didn't ask the same questions. The man looked tired of being stonewalled.

"How do you like it here?" the doctor asked.

"I like it just fine," Peter said. "It's nice not to have to worry about food."

"Peter, you've been starving, haven't you?" the psychiatrist said. "Forgetting to eat?"

Was it his imagination, or was the doctor tearing up? Peter was making a grown man cry. How could the man cry so easily? Peter wasn't sure if he should feel guilty for making him cry, or if he should congratulate himself for beating the enemy. No, not the enemy, he reminded himself. As for him, Peter was done crying. He was beyond crying. He hurt so badly he couldn't cry anymore.

"It's been a long day," the psychiatrist said, rubbing his eyes. Peter wondered if he had lost someone, too.

"It reminds me of college, this place, like a dormitory," Peter said, strangely cheerful. "Even the furniture looks the same."

"Peter, you're a lot better now, physically. We'd like you to stay in the psych unit just until we get a few things figured out. How much of this is head trauma versus other issues. We'd like to help you some more. Will you sign this form, so we can help you for another week?"

He signed the form like an obedient child. The words didn't make much sense to him anyway, except for the word voluntary. He liked that word. Like he was a volunteer committing some kind of community service.

"What's wrong with me, doc?" Peter said. "I'm not wired right, am I?"

"I'm going to give you some medication that's going to rewire you," the doctor said.

"What's it for?" Peter asked. "What's my diagnosis?"

"It's too early to give you a diagnosis," the doctor said. "It doesn't really matter. What matters is that we get you the right medication."

"Labels don't matter," Peter murmured. He was sure he was repeating something he had heard before. "But I have a right to know what's wrong with me." His voice rose.

"It's too early to say. In the meantime, we'd like to take your pen away, just as a precaution. We consider you a suicide risk."

"Take away my pen, take away my life!" Peter shouted. "You can't take it away. I need to write the stories down. I don't know if she ever wrote them all down."

"You need to rest, Peter," the doctor said gently. "You aren't sleeping much."

"Well, you aren't helping much, asking me questions that get me upset right before I'm supposed to go to sleep."

The doctor took off his glasses and rubbed his eyes. "I'm sorry to bother you, Peter. It's just that we need a little more time to get things sorted out, so we can help you get better."

After the psychiatrist left the room, Peter got up and walked slowly down the corridor. The hallway smelled of bleach and the floor shined under the fluorescent lighting. One of the nurses gave him a soft look. "You should be in bed, Peter," she said. "You need your rest."

"You're right," he said, leaning over the counter. She didn't notice he had taken her pen. He went back to his room to continue the story. He wondered briefly if writing was its own form of mental illness. If there were a pill to get him to stop writing, would he take it?

The nurse came and knocked on the door, and he hid the pen under his mattress. His roommate didn't say a word, an accomplice to the crime. Peter couldn't remember the nurse's name. It was a blur. She was the blond one.

"I've got your meds for you," she said, handing him two large pills in a small plastic cup and another Styrofoam cup full of water.

"I don't want them," he said. "I don't trust pills."

"Peter, you need these to get better," she pleaded. "It's not like the movies. I can't force you to take them. All I can do is ask. Please take them. They'll help you."

She handed him an information sheet. It listed a long string of foreign sounding names and words. Used for the treatment of epilepsy and mood disorders, he read. I don't have epilepsy, he thought. Why didn't the doctor just put a name to the damn thing? Mood disorder. It made him wonder about the ups and downs. It was more like a sleep disorder in his mind. He didn't remember the last time he had slept for more than a few hours. Each time they took his blood pressure, it had skyrocketed. His body seemed to have too much adrenaline. He was sweating bullets and wasn't thinking clearly anymore. He knew that. It seemed like he went in and out. He kept forgetting things and remembering them later. The stories flitted in and out of his mind. He remembered the story about his grandfather with dementia. Was this like that? Was this the same feeling? The hard things were easy. The easy things were hard.

He held the cup in his hand. He held it and looked down at the pills, long and white. Would he take them? Should he take them? Tossing them all in his mouth at once, he swallowed them and wiped his mouth. He felt like Alice in Wonderland, so very small, so very large.

The hospital room was dark except for a small, yellow light coming from the outlet. The darkness reminded him of being in the womb. Peter imagined his mother's heartbeat, felt his own. He told himself this was a peaceful place; there was no reason to be afraid. He curled into the fetal position in his hospital bed. A strange tingling shot through his arms and legs, through his very blood. It must be the medicine, he thought. His brain felt scrambled. When he squeezed his eyes shut, images shot through his mind, distorted, flickering, flashing, memories, pieces of art, green bright white flashes of stars, all sorts of little things.

He turned over in bed and opened his eyes and then he saw him, a figure, a dark figure that seemed fuzzy at first but slowly snapped into focus. Peter rubbed his eyes, but the figure still was there, crouching at his bedside.

"Are you a ghost?" Peter asked softly. He didn't want to wake Max, who was snoring on the other side of the curtain.

"Maybe," the man said. He was weathered. His hair had turned silver but it was short now, short and respectable, a bit corporate actually.

"Who are you?" he asked.

"I'm you from another time."

Peter reached out and touched the man's face. The skin felt rough and stubbly. He could feel the tingle on his own skin when he touched the man. A shiver ran through him. They were connected somehow. This man was real, as real as anything anyway.

"Why are you here?" he asked.

"So that you don't lose hope," the other Peter said. "You have a responsibility to live."

"Why?" he asked. "Why do I have to live?"

"For her," the man said.

"That doesn't make any sense."

"Since when did you ever make sense?"

Peter laughed, and the older man laughed in unison and the sound had a strange echoing feel to it. It reminded him of his brother, the way their voices mingled, indistinguishable from one another when they spoke at once.

"I know now is a rough time, but it will get better," the man said.

"How do you know that?" Peter sat up in bed and crossed his arms, clutching them tightly in the dark.

"Because I've seen it. I've lived it. The world is a beautiful place, and you have a place in it."

"I keep losing track of time," Peter said, motioning to his clothes. He kept forgetting to change them. "The pills make me sleepy."

"Time doesn't matter," the man said. "You can learn to live without it."

"I'm crazy, aren't I?" Peter asked.

"There's nothing wrong with crazy," the man said. "I'd rather be crazy than normal. Normal people are sheep. They're afraid of people thinking they're crazy, so they never step out of line. You're free, free to do whatever you want, to wander wherever you want."

"What should I do then, when I get out of here?" Peter asked.

"You have itchy feet, always have, so why don't you travel the world?"

"Never stop moving," Peter murmured. "That's what I'll do."

"I have to go now," the man said. "The nurses will be coming soon to check on you. You'll be fine. You just have to accept a few things first."

Peter stood up shakily. His arms and legs felt sluggish, like he was supposed to be asleep.

"It's the medication," the man said, reading his mind. "Sometimes it makes you feel worse before you feel better. Goodbye, Peter."

"Goodbye, Peter," Peter said.

Peter tried not to view the psychiatrist as an adversary, as an enemy, but at the same time it was hard to trust him. After all, the man thought he was crazy. Not that the psychiatrist would ever use those words. He wouldn't even tell Peter what was wrong with him exactly. Maybe he didn't know or maybe he didn't want to say anything negative, but Peter didn't like it. It occurred to him that the doctor was not God, that he was trying the best he could to help, but Peter still wanted answers.

"Have you ever had a hallucination?" the doctor asked.

"I don't know," Peter said, thinking of the old man who visited in the dark. He wondered if Max had told the doctor about him mumbling in the night. "I had a dream last night I thought was real, and I felt like my blood was burning. Does that count as a hallucination?"

"Yes," the doctor said. "Have you ever heard voices?"

"Don't think so," Peter said. Sometimes, when he was falling asleep, he imagined someone calling his name softly. Peter, Peter. No, that didn't count. He was sure everyone heard things like that in their sleep.

"Tell me about the girl in the car," the doctor said.

"The woman in the car," Peter corrected. "Don't be a misogynistic prick." What was he saying? The truth? He had no filter, things just poured out of his mouth. Was it the medication? It filled him with a small amount of horror.

The psychiatrist barely flinched. Perhaps he was used to it.

"She was lovely," he said. "She was one of the loveliest people I've ever met. Except for the fact that she hit me with her car. But I guess that wasn't really her fault."

"I hear you've been writing about her," the doctor said.

"Not really about her per se, just the stories she told me, the stories we told each other to pass the time in the snowstorm. You see, it's the only way to keep her alive."

"But she isn't alive," the doctor said, putting the tips of his fingers together to form a tent with his hands, massive hands. Strong hands, white and covered with blue veins that rose like ridges. Maybe he was older than Peter first had thought.

"I know that," Peter snapped. "But she had this thing about her stories, that through them she could live forever."

"Do you believe that?" the doctor said, blinking a few times.

"I don't know," Peter said. "But it can't hurt to tell them."

"But it can hurt, Peter," the doctor said. "If you can't let them go. If you can't let her go."

"I barely knew her," Peter said. The last thing he was going to do was confess to this man. It was a secret. She'd never know. He'd never know.

"Peter, do you care to tell me why you were out there in that snowstorm?"

"No, I don't want to tell you."

"It's because you needed help, wasn't it?"

"I don't need anyone's help," Peter said. "I'm fine."

"You are most certainly not fine," the doctor said. "I've talked at length to the social worker. The nurses have told me your stories. That bit about the bank, there was some truth to it, wasn't there?"

"Just one part," Peter said.

"They never filed any charges against you, Peter," the doctor said. "They never thought you did it. You were being paranoid."

Peter felt his mouth go dry as cotton.

"And what about Elizabeth, do you want to get in contact with her, to let her know you're here?"

"She won't care," Peter said. She's forgotten me, so I've forgotten her, he thought.

"How do you know?" the doctor said.

"No one sends flowers to the psych ward," Peter said sharply.

"That's not true," the doctor said. "Some do."

"It's rare. Admit it," Peter said. "Besides, I don't care about Elizabeth anymore."

"Let me get this straight. You got in trouble with your job, you lost your girlfriend, you were wandering around in a blizzard hoping to die, and you don't care anymore?"

"Not really," Peter said. "But I'm not suicidal, not anymore."

"Why is that?" the doctor asked.

"Because of her," Peter said. "Julie. I have to live for her, because she can't live."

"Do you feel guilty about Julie's death?" The doctor asked.

Peter looked up at the wall, at the round clock in its glass case and wondered when the doctor would move on to the next patient. Time's got to be up, he thought.

"Look, if I hadn't jumped in front of her car," he said. "If I hadn't…" He couldn't finish the sentence. He choked on the words.

"It's not your fault," the doctor said.

"You're a liar," Peter said with a bitter smile. "You tell pretty, little lies to make people feel better."

The doctor left, and Peter read The Book of Impossibility. The days blurred together. Lunch came. Dinner came. Breakfast came. Lights switched on. Lights switched off. Trays came and went, cartons of milk, juice, and steak under the pink plastic covers on pink plastic trays.

But he didn't recognize a single story from the book the nurse had given him. In fact, they weren't stories. They were card tricks. It had to be the wrong book. Images of kings, queens and jacks of spades.

Write what you remember, the nurses kept telling him. So he grabbed his pen and paper. They had given up on taking away his pen. They seemed to embrace the idea now.

"What's the difference between brain damage, a brain injury, dementia, and a chemical imbalance?" He wondered out loud to his roommate Max. "What's the difference?" he asked.

"When it all boils down to it?" Max said. He wheeled his chair to the window and looked out. "Stigma. The old person with dementia is treated with some kind of dignity, most of the time.

"There is no line separating the physical and psychological, not that we've discovered," Max said. "In the East, they talk about a mind body connection. Here's it's compartmentalized, specialized, disconnected, and dissected, like an orchestra stripped of its various parts and sections and told to play together anyway."

"Are you a philosopher?" Peter asked.

"I like to read them," Max said, pointing to a copy of Plato's Allegory of a Cave on his nightstand right next to the Bible.

"How did you break your leg?" Peter asked.

"I fell out of a window and landed six stories down," Max said. His gaze was still transfixed outside, searching the pale blue sky.

"Why did you fall?"

"No reason," Max said.

"There has to be a reason."

"That's the thing, there wasn't any 'reason.' I wasn't reasonable. You're one to talk, walking into the middle of a snowstorm and jumping in front of a car."

"I didn't have any place to go. So you're a philosopher, then?" Peter said, pointing to Plato, changing the subject. "What's in that book?"

"It's the story of these people who grow up in a cave and think the shadows on the wall cast by objects against the light of the fire are real. And then they go up above the ground, and they discover sunlight, and they can see the objects around them. But when they go back to the others and tell them, the others don't believe it. It's all about perception versus reality, you know, the kind of stuff crazy people like me like to deal with."

"Sounds good to me," Peter mumbled. "Maybe Plato was crazy too. Do you think I'm really crazy? Sometimes I wonder if the girl in the car was even real? Or just a character I invented to get through hard times?"

Oh, the disorder of it all, he thought. So he started to write. The tears mixed with ink. Sometimes there were no tears. He was just crying ink. When the pen stopped, the tears started again. And when he was done writing them he wondered which stories were hers and which were his. The words just bled together in his head. And she was a stranger, and it was impossible.

Peter wondered if he were trying to bring her back from the dead, breathe the life back into that chest, blow up her coat like a balloon, reinflate her. He was a psychic after all, not a perfect one, but he could commune with the dead in his own way.

"It's my fault she's dead," he said.

"Maybe. Maybe not," Max said. "I'm tired of reading Plato's Cave. Can I read your stories?"

Peter let Max read them. He was nervous about it, so nervous he bit his nails, fidgeted, and had to leave the room when Max was reading. He spent days in the rec room, putting together puzzles, trying not to play with his bandages. Julie was dead, and her stories had been entrusted to a crazy man. He wondered how she would feel about that.

"I like it," Max said, handing back the notebook. "But I gotta ask you why did you jump in front of the car? Why did you walk into the middle of a snowstorm? What happened?"

"You know that story about Peter Rabbit?" Peter said. "Some of it was true. Not the part about the gunshot or the stolen truck, but the part about the bank. I was fired. I couldn't pay my bills, and after Elizabeth left me, I wanted to die. I was suicidal."

"Oh," Max said. "And what about now?"

Peter hesitated for a moment. He knew this was why they had him in the psych ward and not the regular ward.

"I changed my mind the moment I saw her face," he said. "It was such a short time we spent together, but it didn't matter. I don't even know what she really thought of me, but it doesn't matter."

"You're suffering from survivor's guilt," Max said. "Aren't you?"

"No shit, Sherlock," Peter said. "I killed a woman. She'd be alive if I hadn't jumped in front of her car."

"You didn't really kill her," Max said. "An accident killed her. You should do all the things she didn't get to do, have a family, grow old."

"Live a long and happy life," Peter said, bitterly. "For her and for me."

· · ·

He asked the nurses to see the book. It seemed to have disappeared.

"There is no book," the blond-haired nurse told him gently. "Just go back to sleep. You aren't well."

"But there is a Book of Impossibility," he said.

"It doesn't exist." She took him by the arm, led him back to bed and switched off the florescent lights.

"But it does," he said.

Anything is possible, he thought. He could hear Max snoring.

As he started to fall asleep, he could see the images flickering in his head; her face cast in the snowlight and her hand clutching the steering wheel, fingers pale from the cold. She had long, shimmering, blond hair hanging under her hat. It looked like tangled silk and he wanted to reach over and stroke it.

Dreams aren't so different from stories, he thought. You go to the same place in your mind, the same destination.

And they were on the plane now, sitting in first class in leather chairs with lowered backs. And he had a tumbler of scotch in his hand with ice clinking against the glass.

"You wanted to be on the same plane of existence, I think," she said with a smile.

"Really?" he said, with a groan. "I wish they'd take a scalpel to my brain. Maybe all the bad memories would be scraped away."

"You have to learn to live in the now," she said.

"How the hell do I do that?" he said.

"Damned if I know," she said, laughing and taking his drink. "Good luck, my friend." She took a swig.

"I would've liked to have loved you," he said. "It would've been so easy. Maybe that's why I couldn't read your fortune. I was too close to love."

"Well, it's impossible now," she said. "You know that. We are traveling in different spheres."

She gave him back his glass of scotch, and he took a gulp.

"I always wanted to fly first class," she said. "I always wanted to see what was on the other side of the mysterious black curtain, and now I have."

The engine hummed softly below them. There were no other passengers.

"It's a dream, isn't it?" he said bitterly.

"Isn't it always?" she said, raising an eyebrow.

"Where did you go, Julie? What really happened?"

"I've been traveling," she said.

"Traveling where?" he asked.

"All over the world and through time and space and the neural pathways of human memory," she said.

"That sounds crazy," he said.

"It is," she said. "A moment is an eternity. Did I ever tell you the story about the dog? The St. Bernard?"

"Tell it to me again," he said.

"It's a true story," she said. "This girl was babysitting this guy's St. Bernard while he was on vacation and it died. And it was a hot Chicago summer and the dead dog started to rot. The cheapest place to cremate it was $200. She didn't have any money or a car, but she had a credit card and was close enough to the El. The dog was hundreds of pounds and so she stuffed it in a suitcase and could just barely close the zipper. One of its paws was sticking out. The Brown Line station had no elevator and she was struggling up the steep, narrow, wooden steps. And this guy offered to help her. 'Thanks so much,' she said. He carried it up and they get to the top right before the train pulled away and he darted inside, the doors slide shut, and she watched him pull away with the suitcase with the dead dog.

"You know why I told you this story?" she said. "A week before the blizzard, my cousin from Mississippi told me the same exact story."

"What happened to the dog?" he asked.

"He's been traveling," she said, pulling a suitcase behind her and stepping into the El train. The doors slid shut. He sat down on the seat next to her. "He wasn't even that special, you know. He was just a dog. I wasn't that special either, but I'm traveling."

"You are special," he said.

"It wasn't your fault," she said. "It would've happened one way or another. It was fate."

"But I believe in free will," he insisted. His voice rose like a child's.

"It's both, my friend," she said. "There's only so much you can do with one or the other."

"I can't forgive myself," he said.

"You did nothing wrong," she said. "You were a friend in a dark time. Leave it at that." It was strange to hear his words in her mouth.

"Distract me," he said. "Please."

"No," she said. "It's time to wake up. You get off at the next stop," she said. "Ditch the baggage about what's real and what isn't. There's truth to any story. The details don't matter."

With that, she kissed him on the lips and he opened his mouth with a gasp, his lips parting like the doors to the train. "Monroe," the automated voice said. "Marilyn Monroe."

And then he stepped onto the wooden platform at the Monroe stop and did his best to forget her. But how do you forget a woman like that?

When he woke up, he wrote down all the stories they told each other. He wrote them one by one, again and again until he almost got them right.

The discharge papers didn't say what was wrong with him exactly, but he took the pills the doctors had prescribed. He took them and things started to focus again. It's a funny thing how a prescription can change your vision, he thought. Reality changes from one moment to the next. A simple prescription can change your perception, like a lens at the optometrist. Do you like one or two better, five or six? The light shines on the letters. We are all just projections, aren't we? He thought as he read the label on the plastic bottle. Isn't it grand when you can play with vision? He was starting to sound like Max.

As for the woman, as for Julie, all the pills in the world couldn't make him forget her. She would live forever on his pages. The details didn't matter. He would get it wrong. It would never be perfect, that wasn't possible, but that wasn't the point. It was just another short story of impossible love.

ABOUT THE AUTHOR

 K.B. Jensen is an award-winning author who has hit the bestseller lists on Amazon, with two novels, *Painting With Fire*, an artistic murder mystery, and *A Storm of Stories*, which handles love, craziness and impossibility. Her latest collection of short stories is *Love and Other Monsters in the Dark*. K.B. lives in Littleton, Colorado, with her family and rescue mutt. She enjoys skiing and writing poetry. A former crime reporter and journalist, K.B. is a publishing expert, editor and teen writing camp director. Her work has appeared in Cherry Magazine, Progenitor, New Feathers Anthology, Hypertext Magazine, and more. For info on upcoming workshops, visit kbjensenauthor.com and sign up for her email newsletter.

If you enjoyed *A Storm of Stories*, please consider leaving a review on Amazon or Goodreads and connecting online. A thousand thanks.

www.kbjensenauthor.com
kbjensen.author@gmail.com

ACKNOWLEDGMENTS

No one ever really writes a book alone. I would like to thank all the people who have been involved with the evolution of this book. Without their help, *A Storm of Stories* would have been an impossibility. I've had the good fortune to know many other talented fiction writers who have helped shape my writing, including Matt Yaeger, Jennifer Bisbing, Anna Joranger, Kayla Gordon and Clayton Smith, among others. I'd like to give a special thanks to my editor, Jennifer Bisbing, who I highly recommend, as well as my many betareaders. I am also grateful to Karen Yaeger, a dear friend who is always there when it matters.

ALSO BY K.B. JENSEN

Painting With Fire, an Artistic Murder Mystery

Love and Other Monsters in the Dark